ROBBIE AND ALICE

Robbie and Alice

Published by The Conrad Press in the United Kingdom 2021

Tel: +44(0)1227 472 874
www.theconradpress.com
info@theconradpress.com

ISBN 978-1-913567-85-9

Printed and bound in Great Britain by Clays Ltd, Elcograf S.p.A

Typesetting and Cover Design by The Book Typesetters,
www.thebooktypesetters.com

The Conrad Press logo was designed by Maria Priestley.

Robbie and Alice

a Tudor adventure

Antony Johnson

FOR MAISIE HOLMES

PROLOGUE

At sea, 1520.

The storm had ended. As the sun strengthened, the ship's crew rigged more sail, repaired damage, talked excitedly of reaching England soon. Bristol soon. Back in time for Easter. For though the storm's wind had shovelled them this way and that, torn the spritsail from the bowsprit and carried the topsail from its top, most blasts had raced them eastwards. Now, utterly exhausted, whenever they could, sailors lingered at the sorted ropeways, exchanged tidings, eased aching limbs. And watched, warily, the girl.

Their watching she did not mind. She was royalty, a princess, twelve summers, thirteen winters old, sent by her father, a New World tribal chief, to bond with England's king. She spoke very few English words – but she carried herself with remarkable poise, misunderstood the crew's unease, believed they gave her as much deference as they did the ship's master. Sometimes more.

Now, without warning, she removed her clothes, let them pile, eye-catching as spring flowers, on the fo'c'sle deck. She stepped away quite naked, not a tremor of shame. In moments she was over the starboard rail and into the sea.

The ship's crew hardly breathed.

Then she was back. She'd swum under the keel, taken hold of a damaged halyard trailing from the poop, climbed on board – from the lee side.

The sailors lowered their eyes. Muttered, dumbfounded. What the girl had done wasn't possible. The ship was moving at five, six knots, the sea remained turbulent. No one could swim with such strength. Only a few could even swim.

Soon afterwards the sailors spoke whisperings linking the girl to witchcraft – more strident talk followed, of the same.

CHAPTER ONE

❦ ———— ◆ ———— ❦

NEAR BRISTOL (1519) – THE YEAR BEFORE

Tearfully, urgently, Alice asked the steward. Then the kitchen maid.

Not single magpies…

Not walking under gallows-ladders…

Or sneezing on the stroke of midnight.

None of these brought more bad luck than seeing a leper.

They said.

Leper. The explanations of steward and kitchen maid rattled, rattled and wouldn't leave. Leper: man, woman, child. With discoloured skin, skin insensitivity, numbness, tenderness, skin loss, facial deformity – toes and fingers withered. Sometimes coming off, the kitchen maid – with a darted, rueful look – said.

Alice's leper had arrived along the dirt road that edged the south wall of the manor house where she lived.

Though she ought not to have seen him.

So it simply wasn't fair, she reasoned. Not at all her fault! For being only eleven years old she rarely ventured out alone. Just the high walled courtyard, and sometimes, if feeling particularly daring, the village – and that was quite enough. So why, why today of all the days… so close to the courtyard too…

And… all because, so unfairly, the courtyard had been unusually quiet. No horses being exercised, no carts unloading – not even a servant to pester. For too many minutes Peg, the dog, had been her only companion. Then Peg wandered off to dig in the mud where the south wall threw its shadow.

Now, in her thoughts, over and over:

She'd crossed the courtyard to keep with Peg, but become cold. Bored. Was then drawn to the door.

The south wall had in it a small, rarely opened door. Two substantial, sliding wooden bolts secured it.

On a whim, she'd tugged back the bolts. Free of them, the door had opened: sunshine nosed in; Peg bounded out.

Peg went fast – after rabbits. Lots there, nibbling spring growth in the scrubby ground between the road and the forest. Lots and lots – until Peg got after them.

Watching her dog, she hadn't noticed the leper.

When she had, the leper was only ten yards off. He emerged from the glare of the low just-spring sun, head hidden in a white hood.

Slits for his eyes in the hood.

The slitted eyes fixed on her, fired nightmare associations: witches, malignant spirits, ghost things. She'd stood petrified.

Until the clang from the shake of his bell arrived like a slap, made her consider the direction of the wind on her cheek, made her realise she was downwind.

And terrified she might catch something, certain that even the smell of a leper could bring death, she'd suddenly jumped back, abandoned Peg, slammed the wall door shut, smashed home the bolts, fled tearfully back to the house.

For a long, long while Alice sat on the bench next to the fire in the middle of the great hall. She made patterns and pictures in the ash with the toe part of her shoe. Little by little, her breathing normalised, her trembling eased.

Making pictures seemed always to help.

And the bench seat next to the fireplace was, for Alice, a claimed sanctuary – a particular safe and favourite spot. Usually, most days, when sitting there her mother let her be; her mother had long since reached the conclusion that this was best.

Her mother crossed the hall purposely to speak to her; suppressed her concern for the strained look on the ghost-pale face.

'You're eleven years old,' said her mother. 'Your father and I have agreed a plan. In three years you shall marry. Next month you'll meet your husband-to-be... Where's Peg?'

Servants were dispatched to find the dog. Then Alice was told that the name of her husband was Robert. That he was still a boy. Though almost two years older than she; almost thirteen.

Alice said, it made not a jot of difference: thirteen or fifty. Or ninety. She didn't want to marry anyone. And wouldn't.

The day came, nevertheless. Robert and parent's first visit.
Tension.

Bustle

Trepidation.

Alice sulked. Wouldn't eat breakfast, wouldn't cooperate. Her mother, exasperated, giving up on the usual threats, resorted to slaps. Though only on Alice's bottom. She took good care not to leave visible marks. For, she thought, Alice would need every advantage. Alice was disappointingly gangly and plain, not at all blessed with the good looks of her other children. But they – four others – were gone and in their graves; Alice wasn't. So the best had to be made of it. She brushed hard at Alice's dark, straight hair. Dabbed hard at the tear smudges. Alice's eyes were dark too, big in her face, presenting often – her mother thought – the look of a deer, startled.

Alice's mother said, 'Without your family you're nothing. Nothing at all.'

'Kat's family aren't making her get married.'

'Kat's family can afford to bide their time. We can't.'

'I don't want money. Most of our tenants are penniless, but at least they get to marry for love.'

'Don't be ridiculous!'

The root of the problem was money. Alice understood that much. When she was a baby, the king had died. He'd been called Henry and his son who came next was called Henry. But they were not at all alike. The first Henry, Henry VII had been replaced by Henry VIII; ruthlessness had replaced steadiness. Or so her father said. Her father, Sir Lionel, had assisted Henry's main money raisers Richard Empson and Edmund Dudley; within three days of Henry VII's death the new king had arrested Richard and Edmund on charges of treason – they were beheaded the following year.

It was just acclamation garnering apparently. New King Henry had done it to help bolster his popularity – her father said. People never like tax gatherers. But Richard and Edmund had done nothing wrong. Not really.

Her father had been arrested too, for a time – and soon after that, their money troubles had begun.

Just this last year, several of their servants – one her best favourite – had been let go. Several horses too. Her father had scarcely been home and when he had he'd been different: the jovial confident ease in him had faded; there was all too often pinched troubledness in his face – of late, a look mirrored in her mother.

Alice continued to sulk when Robert and his parents arrived. As he made his greeting bow, rather pompously she thought, she pursed her lips disapprovingly tight, and gave him the look she knew she was expert at – the withering one her mother claimed was so sour it could turn fresh milk to off.

He continued to smile.

She hated his smile.

As they began to eat he smiled at her again. It was self-satisfied, smug, she thought. Of course he had much to be smug about. By marrying into her family, his would raise up into respectability. His family were only merchants, grubbing around in trade. But, apparently, they weren't bothered about a dowry. They had money enough and a deal had been struck. The marriage would be advantageous to both families.

After the meal, Alice and Robert were ushered out into the courtyard to talk and get to know one another better. It was May – but bitterly cold with the wind coming from the north. There was no sun.

'Call me Robbie,' Robert said, breezily. 'No one who knows me calls me Robert. What shall I call you?'

She hissed, 'I'm Alice. And I don't want to talk to you.'

'Let's walk then. Show me the village.'

'No. We'll go this way.'

For she didn't want the villagers to see him with her. It would be too belittling. Everyone, she thought, probably knew why he was there. Word spread fast. So no, not the village. She decided to go through the south-wall door, cross the road, and head towards the forest.

As she opened the door she felt a shock go through her. She hadn't thought she had it in her to be so coldheartedly devious. They could, after all, just go back into the house. But, she thought, there was a good chance that if they went towards the forest he'd forge ahead – and then, just perhaps, some lingering evil from the leper would worm into him. Or... maybe, he'd be devoured by wolves – except that there probably weren't any now. Still, plenty of other menace that might take him down in a forest: vagrants, criminals, elves, fairies, goblins, runaway dancing-bears...

She never, usually, went far – there.

They stood on the dirt road, stared into the tree press. Robbie put his hand in his doublet and pulled out a tightly rolled piece of paper – big: over a foot long. 'You should look at this,' he said.

'What is it?'

'A map'

'A map!'

'There's a bird called a parrot that does that.'

'What?'

'Repeats things you say.'

'Never heard that.'

'No?'

Robbie had stepped very close to her. There was something threatening in his closeness.

Arrogance – was most definitely the word that most summed him up, she thought. Arrogance. A show-offs' arrogance.

He was saying (arrogantly), 'It's not just girls who don't know lots of stuff. In the last thirty years there have been massive things that everyone didn't know that now they do. So we just have to be ready to discover – what do you think?'

While he'd been talking, he'd unrolled the map and shoved it in front of her face. 'I drew it with pen and ink,' he said. 'Then painted on the colour. That's the town where I live. There's the river and the harbour. Those bits there are the hills and those, marshlands that go eastwards for miles.'

Alice forced herself to look. And, reluctantly, became interested. She liked the way he'd drawn the town, it was like the view a bird would have looking down, but not right above, not straight down. It – the bird – was away off to one side, at the edge where the river met the sea. There was a monster drawn in the sea. She liked that too. But she wasn't going to say so.

'If you live where you live you don't need a map,' she said sniffily.

He placed his hands on her shoulders, fixing her eyes with his – eyes that were, she thought, laughing at her, mocking her. He said, 'I drew it to practise, because one day I'm going to make great discoveries of exploration and make maps of the places I discover. I'll be known far and wide as Robbie the fearless adventurer.'

'No one is ever really fearless.'

'I am.' And he crossed the road, and began to walk purposefully, big strides, along a narrow track that led off through the scrub grass towards the trees.

Alice followed, momentarily forgetting that her plan was for Robbie to enter the forest alone. Angry, irritated, stung by his bravado, she thought: I can be brave too.

Suddenly it mattered that he'd think she was.

When the track reached the trees it shrank. The trees squeezed up tight to it almost at once. But she was sure it would go on: the village children tasked with taking pigs into the forest to feed on acorns, roots, anything – pigs would eat anything – had made it.

Though she kept her distance from those children.

Quickly Robbie was almost out of sight, pressing ahead. 'Keep up,' he shouted back cheerfully.

Quite soon, the track went on with less certainty: brambles, branches, undergrowth of all sorts overgrowing it. They had to step over fallen branches, and break through bushy stuff. Probably, Alice thought, the children with the pigs didn't go in this deep – not very often.

Robbie waited for her. 'Should have brought my sword,' he said.

'You shouldn't have a sword. You're not old enough and you're not a gentleman's son.'

'I'll be a gentlewoman's husband once I marry you. I can wear a sword.'

'You're not to talk about it.'

'Swords?'

'Marriage.'

Robbie turned away from her and continued walking. Alice kept closer. Most of the time she kept her eyes fixed firmly on his legs. She didn't much want to look around – and if she looked up she could barely see the sky; the tree foliage, although it was only May, was already thick enough to obscure most of it. It was like being at the bottom of a murky river, she thought. And she didn't like that; sometimes she had scarily bad dreams in which she was with creatures at the bottom of some river. Or sea.

Sometimes, just above her, a bird darted. That made her heart thud even more, and the branches of the trees creaked and rubbed in the wind with a terrible strangeness at times. She thought she glimpsed eyes too: creatures, things watching. But she didn't look closely; she didn't dare.

'I think we've come far enough,' she said desperately.

'No. Not if we're explorers. Like Columbus. Like Cabot.' He gave her an interrogating look. 'You do know about Columbus?'

'Yes.' She lied.

'Tell me.'

'I don't have to.'

'It's because you don't.'

'No, it's because I don't have to.' Tears came up into her eyes. She prided herself on knowing a lot of things. She was inquisitive by nature her mother said. She was humiliated that she hadn't heard of this Columbus person – or the other one. 'I'm going back now,' she said.

'Then you'll go without me.'

The tears were suddenly very obvious. 'Don't be a baby,' he said – then tempered it with a note of kindness. 'Look, when I get home I'll draw a map of what we've discovered. I'll send it to you.'

'There's nothing to discover,' she sobbed.

'There will be. Come on.'

He didn't seem at all put out by her crying. He set off again, jauntily, a length of strong branch in his hand with which he beat back any undergrowth that looped over the track.

She let him go.

As he disappeared she shouted, 'We should be back in the house by now.'

He stopped. 'How do you know? Do you know what the time is?'

She didn't – unfortunately. Usually when she was outdoors she kept track of the time by listening out for the monastery's bell. It was nearly a mile away, the monastery, isolated because it was run by Cistercian monks who, unlike the more numerous Benedictine's, liked to live in remote spots, far from other people. Nevertheless, the wind, when blowing from the direction it most often did, carried the sound of its bell to Alice's village. It rang every day without fail, marking the time for prayer: vigils, matins, prime, tierce, sext, nones, vespers, compline. But this afternoon, though she was sure the wind was right, she hadn't once heard it.

Strange!

There was no sun to help either.

Fighting back the tears, she caught up with him. 'I know it's late,' she said.

'And I know our journey's only just begun. Look.'

Robbie stepped to one side, pushing into a bush so that she could see past him. The track suddenly, she saw, ended; the ground fell away. It was because of a stream, she realised going closer. A small stream that cut across.

The track continued on the other side though. They only had to jump over.

'Take off your shoes,' said Robbie.

'I jump better with them on.'

'We'll follow the stream. See where it leads.'

'What! Why would we want to do that?'

'Do you know where it goes?'

'No.'

'There you are then.'

'I'm tired of this game.'

'Exploring isn't a game.'

Robbie pulled off his shoes and stockings and scrambled down the bank into the water. The water was less than knee deep; the bank at a height level with his chest.

'Hurry up,' he said to Alice.

Alice hitched up her skirt, removed her shoes, and slid reluctantly down, hating it.

The water wasn't as cold as she'd expected – and the soft mud that her feet sank into wasn't so very bad either. But sometimes there were stones, and sometimes watery plants that wrapped around her legs in the current. And the smell from the bank was nasty: damp, rotten, wet-doggish. It was like the smell of most of the villagers' houses.

The worst thing though was that it was much darker being in the stream bed than on the track; the trees and plants pressed in even tighter; she felt surrounded, suffocated.

'How long are we going to follow this for?' she called. Again, Robbie was well ahead.

'Until we arrive of course.'

'Arrive where?'

'Bound to be somewhere.'

'Talk sense.'

'Talking sense is going to be my life's work.'

'Really!'

Alice fell silent and turned her mind back to ways to get out of the marriage. Because he was insufferable; too awful for words!

In recent days she'd considered all sorts, from running away from home (that'd teach them) to poison – poisoning him that was; not her. Of course, just possibly, when her parents found out where he'd taken her they'd be appalled enough to begin a great row that might end it all anyhow. They hated her being exposed to the slightest risk. Her three brothers had died; her sister too. She was the only surviving child.

So she should stay out as long as he wanted to, she suddenly decided. The longer the better, she thought.

'This is fun,' she said.

'See. I knew you'd enjoy it eventually.'

Then she slipped and fell. One moment her legs were solidly splashing along, then they went from under her and she was falling backwards into the stream. Her head went right back too. Her shoes came out of her hands. She sank into muddy slime. All of her soaked.

When she stood up again she screamed.

He waded back. He found her shoes. He laughed.

'I hate you,' she wailed.

'You don't.'

'Mummy'll kill me.'

'Really?'

'Pretty close.'

She flinched, seeing a picture of Mummy in her mind's eye, sharp as if in a Venetian mirror: spitting-cross, arm raised to strike. And Mummy'd be even crosser with Robbie, she thought. For certain.

And then she thought: now she really might not have to marry him – not ever! She was shivering, her teeth were chattering, but she was suddenly the most hopeful she'd been all day. Mummy would hate him too. She straightened, suppressed a shudder. 'Let's just keep going,' she said.

He led on, but made a noticeable effort to go more slowly, pause and wait whenever she fell behind. And when he did – stop, looked back – she flashed him a sweet smile, while muttering under her breath, I hate you, hate you, hate you. Each time: a smile and three hates. A sort of ritual; helping her move.

She thought a lot about how much she was hating him. She decided, more than anyone ever before... Ever.

The stream was widening. And it was wandering, bending more. Suddenly, with a stab of horror, it came to her that she knew where it might end. Not that she'd ever been there.

Some of the village children had, or said they had. It wasn't a place you were encouraged to go. It was a haunted place. An evil place. A place welcoming to devils.

Her heart sank.

Her unease increased minute by minute.

The stream's changes now shouted in her head: the stream was wriggling more and the slope of its banks was often not as steep; tree roots were less exposed; there was more undergrowth at its edge; the foliage above seemed thinner and the light penetrated in wider shafts; there were many more flowers: blue ones, white ones, yellow ones... When they rounded the biggest bend so far, everything opened out strangely – it was, she thought, as if the forest had been pulled open by giant hands and pegged back, purposely revealing a lake.

Sort of lake. But small; too small for what she thought a lake must be; too big for a pond. Or a moat.

Even a very wide moat, she decided. Though it was moat-ish – because in the middle was an island with buildings, clustered in an L-shape. Except – well, buildings once; now they were ruins, though the biggest one still had a recognisable tower. Much like a church's. Or indeed her own house – though there, the main building adjoining the tower was made of timber, not stone, and was lived in. No one had lived here for a hundred years.

She was numbingly scared.

She rushed to get right up to Robbie. The fear drove her to clutch Robbie's arm. 'This is as far as we go,' she said. 'We never should have come here.'

CHAPTER TWO

———◇———

THE LETTER

He was astonished that a letter arrived. He hadn't seen her for a year. He didn't expect to see her again until much closer to the wedding, quite possibly not until the very day. He certainly didn't think she'd write – plus, most of the girls he knew didn't know how.

Best beloved explorer, it began (encouraging start, he thought). I need help. Your particular help. You are the only one I can think of that I should ask. You must find a reason to visit. Just you. You will need to stay for a few days. I'll explain when I see you. I don't want to write the reason down. But some of it has to do with a map, and I know you're good with maps.

She didn't sign off with anything affectionate. He'd have been stunned if she had.

Their last meeting, which was still their first, had ended badly. Both sets of parents had been daggers-drawn cross. And when Alice's mother had chastised her for getting so wet, so filthy, she said that he'd pushed her, maliciously pushed her so she went under.

'I didn't,' he protested.

'I might have drowned.'

'But I didn't push you. It's a lie.'

'Then why would Alice say it,' said Alice's mother. 'Alice doesn't ever tell lies.'

'We've brought her up to always be truthful,' said Alice's father.

'Robbie's horrid. He's horrid,' said Alice. And when Robbie stared incredulously at her, a spark of triumph met it.

After he opened the letter, read Alice's every word twice, he sat holding it for a long time, dazed. His fingers kept on tracing the wax indentations of the broken seal; he was more than usually weary. His day at school was long: six o'clock start, five o'clock finish, with just the briefest of breaks and very strict discipline. Unusually, the schoolmaster's birch hadn't whacked him today. He'd kept utterly focused. Though staying focused – on tasks mostly to do with Latin (reading it, writing it, reciting it) – was always, for him, difficult to maintain. But today he had – because he'd promised his mum last night, as he'd made ready for bed, that he'd make more effort. And today, he'd got through without a single new bruise. Worked hard. Not at all surprising that he was dog-tired now.

Mum had handed him the letter the moment he'd returned from school. He'd spluttered, said he'd read it outside, that he needed a breath of air. He half-ran out, then ran fast. His house was at the top of a road that led directly down to the quayside. The evening breeze, he reasoned, should be coming in off the sea and the smells carried on it he always found stimulating. Very much the right sort of place to open a troubling letter.

For Bristol, where he lived, was one of the busiest ports in England. Seafaring had recently moved to the cutting edge of wealth and adventure. His parents, as merchants, were greatly involved.

And so would he be – soon. One more year of school and then he'd be allowed to go and sail to distant lands to help promote his parents' business. It was a promise made to him by his mum and his dad. Finish school, go to sea – and marry Alice.

He still wasn't sure why he had to marry Alice. But he knew it too was 'business'.

He looked again at the letter. For a long while he let his fingers trail along the loops of Alice's words. The up-downness of the lettering was erratic and there had been blotting. Her handwriting wasn't a patch on his own, he thought. He pictured offering her lessons, found the fury in her face.

He hadn't imagined she'd ever write to him willingly. It was obvious she didn't want to become his wife. Her problem, her need to see him, must be serious.

His dad said, 'You had a letter?'

His mum said, 'I've been waiting all day to hear what's in it.'

'It's from Alice,'

'I know that. The man who came with it explained that much.'

'She wants to see me. Can I go?'

'Show us the letter?'

'I can't. I went down to the harbour to read it. I watched a caravel unloading. Just in from Portugal it was. The caravel. A really good-looking ship, Mum – just the sort you like. I was watching them unload and a gust of wind snatched Alice's letter out of my hand and into the water. I lost it.'

'That was very careless.'

They hadn't, he knew, believed him for a moment. It was a stupid lie. The wind was coming in off the water. Dad would have realised; Mum too probably. But they'd pretended to believe him – after one of those knowing glances at each other that parents always seem to make. No doubt they thought Alice had written to him about love and that he was too embarrassed to say.

It was a two-day journey to Alice's house. The roads were not especially safe for a lone traveller. When, after a week of trying, Robbie's dad secured the agreement of merchants who were going in the right direction and willing to let Robbie, for a small fee, tag along, his dad's face split into a grin that stretched from ear to ear, and his mum – clasping Robbie's hands – danced a jig.

The week passed ridiculously slowly. Robbie couldn't keep his thoughts on his schoolwork; he was birched most days. When the time to go finally arrived, his mind was in so much of a whirl that he left the house without his luggage and had to go back for it. The merchants waited impatiently. There were six of them. They were by the quayside, having finished loading onto mules the cargo they had bought off the ship

26

moored there. 'Time is money,' said the first man Robbie's dad apologised to. 'Daylight is safety,' said the next. 'It won't do to be out in the dark.'

'Say you're sorry,' Robbie's dad urged. But Robbie had moved away and was looking at the ship.

It had been to the Med, Dad had said, run the gauntlet of the warlike Turks and returned laden with sugar, hides and ginger. It was called 'Merlin'. But that was all he knew; Bristol wasn't its home port.

'Anytime today would be good,' said the merchant's leader, sarcastically, thrusting his pox-marked, scarred face close enough for Robbie to smell bad breath.

'I hope someone loosens off those warps soon,' said Robbie.

'You'd know best I suppose,' said the man.

'Oh yes,' said Robbie.

'Cocksure little so-and-so ain't cher.'

'No I'm not. Surely you know that the tide races away here. It's the biggest drop in the country. Thirty feet sometimes. She'll be beached in no time. Ship-shape Bristol fashion is not an idle saying to a ship mooring here.'

'What I know is the wind's strengthening, a storm's likely coming and the pack mules are restless. And because of you, we're late.'

The rain arrived and fell heavily before they cleared the town. The streets, which were narrow and filled with mud and garbage-filth, quickly puddled. As the hooves of the mules stirred the mud it let out sickening stench. Robbie, walking behind a mule, hunched into his coat. The tightly packed wooden-frame houses flanking the streets seemed determined to bully him; water poured off their projecting upper floor roofs in streams that were hard to avoid.

He quickly became soaked, cold and miserable. It had been a rotten start. He mouthed prayers to Saint Christopher that it would get better.

The attack came an hour into their next day's travel. It was made by ten or so vagrants, armed with longbows, axes, pikes. They went for the rear pack mule, tried to isolate it, run back into the forest with it.

Robbie was near the mule they wanted. He'd been made to walk at the back. No one had wanted to walk with him. Last night, when they'd camped, they'd paid little attention to his needs.

Up until then, yesterday's rain had followed them. This morning, because of the ground-wet, and white mist coming, going, coming, like puffed chill-breath, everything stayed damp – and Robbie miserable. The mist held at the woodland's edge when the sun manoeuvred to roll it back.

Half a mile after a small village, just as all traces of cultivated land disappeared, the woodland squeezed closer than it should. Several arrows loosed out of its haze. The merchant walking beside the rear pack mule took two arrows in his chest and crumpled down. Robbie ran over, grabbed the mule's harness and tried to make it go faster; get with the others.

From behind a tree a man jumped out, inches from Robbie. Robbie tried to react but the man's fist struck him hard in the stomach. As he doubled up, the same fist struck his mouth. Blood filled his throat. He fell, rolled desperately – the mule almost trampling him. And his attacker was almost away with it. But Robbie flung up an arm, got a grip on one of the pannier baskets and clung on. Robbie slowed the mule; worked to give his fellow travellers time.

Now there was fighting all around Robbie. Some of the merchants had swords. They were forcing the attackers back. Robbie was still clinging to the mule. Robbie saw the group's pox-scarred leader lunging with his sword at a great hulk of an axeman. When the man brought the axe up to parry the sword, a dagger was thrust under the axe shaft and into the axman's belly. He screamed and went down.

And then it was over. Over with much the same suddenness with which it began. The robbers lost heart, fled.

Pox-face said, 'They'd like as not 'ave got clean away with that mule if you hadn't clung on. Well done.'

CHAPTER THREE

THE STRANGER

He told Alice about his part in rescuing the mule at once. The moment he arrived. Proudly. Before they were through the door.

'Typical,' she snapped. 'Can you never say anything without boasting about yourself?'

'I'm just saying.'

'You just don't get it do you.'

Well she hasn't changed, Robbie thought. But then, quite quickly, and with a strange feeling that seemed to deposit the oddest ache in his stomach, he saw that in one sense anyway she had: she was taller, still gangly (willowy, was how his mum put it), but her face had become sort of pretty; there was more definition – her thin pale face, framed by dark-coloured, down-to-the-shoulders hair, had developed an odd, lopsided prettiness. Her big dark eyes dominated – right now, determined as ever to mock him.

He wondered if he'd ever seen her smile.

The hall was the manor house's biggest room. In its middle

was a hearth. At her insistence they sat down close to it, on a bench. He waited expectantly. Why on earth did she need to see him?

He gave her a hard stare. She ran her hand distractedly through her hair, but said nothing. Her hair was tidier too, he thought. Much more so than that last time. Which was more than could be said for the room. It wasn't tidy at all. And the fire on the hearth was surprisingly meagre, giving off a lot of smoke. Beneath his feet the straw was stale, dirtied. No fresh woodland flowers added to perk it.

Robbie looked around more observantly, wondering if the lack of domestic care was significant, some sort of clue as to why he was there. Alice didn't seem in a hurry to say. When Peg wandered over and gave them a pathetic dog stare, Alice muttered something about finding a servant and left.

In essence, the house probably wasn't any different from what he remembered; the hall had been scarcely furnished then and it still was: just the long dining table, benches, one cupboard and the one rather threadbare wall tapestry. The other rooms might be more welcoming of course; beyond the head of the table were two doors, which led, respectively, to the kitchen and the parlour – and from the parlour you could reach the stone tower. But Robbie hadn't ever been further than the hall, so he didn't know how they were rigged out. He did know that access to all upstairs rooms not in the tower was by ladder; there was no modern staircase. His parents' house had a staircase.

They had glass in the windows too.

And when Alice returned he was about to say so – and only just didn't.

'Codfish,' she said.

'What?'

'You opened your mouth and nothing came out.'

'Well. It's your fault. You told me not to boast.'

'Your boasting is not my fault.'

Silence once more. Sitting side by side, stiff and awkward, not looking at each other. Robbie making a fuss of Peg.

A servant brought a jug of ale and two cups. When the servant went Robbie said, 'Where are your parents?'

'Mummy's upstairs. My father…' She faltered. Her face puckered. Tears came into her eyes.

'What's happened? You have to tell me. You've made me come all this way.'

She didn't answer. She was struggling to find some control. Her lips were trembling.

Robbie didn't know how best to respond. He didn't have any sisters. He wasn't often alone with girls.

He poured the ale into the two cups. 'Thirsty,' he said.

She sniffed and said sarcastically, 'Being a hero is thirsty work.'

'Have you dragged me here just to insult me?'

'I might have.'

'But you didn't?'

'No.'

While he was drinking down his second cup she wiped away any remaining tears with her sleeve, stood up and suggested they walk to the village. 'I meant today, not tomorrow,' she added, when he didn't immediately move.

'From what I remember you don't much like to go to the village.'

'It's just that I thought you could ask the villagers.'

'Ask them what?'

'If there's another way to get to it.'

'Get to where, for heaven's sake?'

'I'll explain when we're in the village.'

He made a derisive grunt and raised his eyes to the roof beams in exasperation. 'I want to know what this is all about now. Why can't you talk to them about whatever it is? They have to take notice of you.'

She stared at him. Her eyes were wide. Beseeching. 'Not here.'

'No. Here. Explain.'

'It's just that you'll do it better than me, that's all.'

'Well, I think it's that you're too scared to – whatever it is.'

She didn't answer.

'Because everything scares you.'

'It doesn't!'

'It really does.'

'Fine!' She walked away from him and then spun angrily back. 'The reason you'll do it better is that you're so arrogant you won't be put off. You're too pig-headed to be put off. You just might find out.'

'Find out what?'

'Just come with me to the village. Please!'

Her village was not much different from the other villages that Robbie had seen. There were about thirty houses, mostly one-roomed, all wattle and daub constructed. And a stone church in the village centre. And two great fields, divided up into strips, where the villagers worked. There was other farmed land and an orchard that belonged to Alice's family too; but from where they were sat they couldn't see any of that.

They were sat next to the stocks, resting their backs against the part where miscreants' legs would be fixed in – happily it hadn't been used for ages, Alice said.

It was a good place to sit, though; the sun had made the wood warm; the May wind was cold and blustery.

'Come on. What's happened?'

She put her thumb in her mouth and sucked it. Her face was very pale.

'Tell me.'

'Daddy's disappeared.'

'What!'

'Mummy doesn't know where he's gone. She's asked people of course. He should have been back. But he hasn't. And…'

She began to cry. Much harder than before. Her shoulders and chest heaved as she sobbed.

Robbie put a hand on her shoulders. She brushed it away.

For a long time she couldn't speak.

Eventually, all in a rush she said, 'The day before I wrote to you, men came looking for him. Came to our house. They were Cardinal Wolsey's men. They thought we'd know where he was. He was supposed to be taking care of someone. They expected him to be here with that someone. But he wasn't. They wanted to question him. They spoke of witchcraft.'

'But you don't know where he's gone?'

'No one who should does. But I think I might. Except that Mummy doesn't believe me. I need you to believe me.'

34

'Go on.'

It had been a day of April gales when she'd last seen her father. Snow and sleet mixed in with rain that day. Branches were ripped from the trees.

Alice had gone to bed early but she'd been unable to sleep. There were too many creaks and bangs. Usually she liked being in bed; liked the security of it: to be snuggled under blankets with her dreams.

Not that night. Every evil thing that could possibly be imagined might have been out in the world that night. She couldn't stop thinking about such things.

And then she'd heard her father's voice, outside the house in the courtyard. No one had said he was coming home. She'd got out of bed and looked out.

She'd only pulled the shutter back a little. But she'd seen him straight away. He was walking across the courtyard, lantern in his hand, not much light. But most definitely it was he. Walking away from John who looked after the stables. John was holding a horse and there was someone else with her father.

She couldn't see who. Not clearly. It was horribly dark. Her father's lantern gave out very little light.

The someone was small. A girl, she thought. Almost certainly. A girl – her sort of age. Possibly.

Possibly...

She only had a fleeting impression of it all. They were gone and away in moments.

But she was sure she knew where they were heading – that they must have gone there.

John denied the whole story and her mother didn't believe her.

John said her father hadn't been there at all.

And the next day, in the stables there was no horse.

No horse!

But she had seen it. She had!

And she believed she knew where her father and companion had gone. Because they were in the courtyard one minute and then not, so they must have left through the courtyard side-exit: the little bolted door. The one she'd used when she saw the leper. The one she'd taken Robbie through when they'd ended up close to the ruins. On the lake. The ruins on the island on the lake.

The island with the ruins was a place her father had quizzed her about – what was there and how did she get to it – just a week before.

'I don't like to remember about it Daddy.'

'I want you to.'

'Must I?'

'It's important. A matter of life or death.'

'Saints preserve us!'

CHAPTER FOUR

———◆———

CREATURES OF THE DEEP

When evening was close and the men came back from their labouring in the fields, Robbie spoke to them. He asked them what Alice wanted to know: were there other ways to get to the ruins on the island, did they know if anyone ever went there, had they taken anyone there recently, had they been there themselves?

Every answer was a 'no'. 'No mistress.' 'No master.' And many of the answers were given with a surly snap, the men's eyes not meeting Robbie's. It was as if they were afraid to talk about the place.

Robbie spoke to some of the village women too. The results were much the same.

Robbie said to Alice, 'If you were too scared to do it, you could have got a servant to do what I've just done. Or your friend Kat. You didn't need me.'

'I suppose,' she said moodily. 'But there's another reason I wanted you to come here. It's because you know about maps.'

She wasn't able to show him the map. When they returned to

the manor house her mother was waiting and the table was laid up for supper.

There was partridge, snipe and pastries. Some wine too. Robbie ate hungrily. Alice ate slowly. Alice's mother hardly ate at all. She was clearly ill at ease – Alice's mother. There was a haunted, far-away look on her face.

Most oddly of all, she hadn't asked him about his journey. Or even about his parents' reaction to Alice's letter – or what he and Alice had been doing all afternoon. She either knew all about Alice's plans, or had become a little insane. Or both!

At first he was too hungry to care.

But eventually, with his plate almost emptied, he remembered that his mum would be really cross if polite conversation wasn't made at mealtimes. So he put down his knife, wiped his fingers and decided to tell the story about the robbery and his part in foiling it. But as he opened his mouth to begin he remembered Alice's complaint about his boasting – and was surprised that he cared. Instead he said, 'My parents send their regards. Their best wishes.'

Alice's mother gave him a quizzical, searching look, as if she'd only just remembered he was sitting there.

'Your parents?'

'Yes. Sorry they couldn't come too. Bristol's shipping ventures go from strength to strength. They are very busy.'

'Bristol. Yes. Rather a dingy, squalid little town. Don't much like to go there. Though it does have a splendid spice shop. For saffron, ginger, that sort of thing. Very expensive. I said to Lionel last time…' Her voice trailed off.

'Sir Lionel is away? Business?' Robbie decided to feign innocence, probe a little.

She didn't answer. After a few moments of awkward silence she said, 'Witches these days? Are usually hanged? Am I right? Not burned? Not in England?'

'Mummy! You promised you wouldn't keep asking that.'

'Did I dear? I just need to be sure.'

When the meal was over and Alice's mother had gone to her room Alice said, 'She keeps banging on about being hanged or burned,' and burst into tears.

Robbie looked around in desperation – for help, because it just wasn't fair. Tears. He hated tears – and this was the third time that day that Alice had blubbed.

Luckily the servant clearing, a girl not much older than Alice, ran over to give comfort. Robbie moved away and began to talk to the steward who was there to supervise the servant.

The steward's name was Tom. He said he'd been in Sir Lionel's service all his life. And that of Sir Lionel's father too.

'That's good, because I want to ask you about something that happened over a hundred years ago.'

'I'm not that old, sir.'

'I know. But you must have heard about it.'

'Ask away!'

～

Robbie awoke to the sun and a cockerel's cry. He was surprised that he'd been asleep. When he'd first gone to bed his thoughts had been in a whirl, and quite soon there'd been the sound of sobbing from Alice's room. And Alice's mum's.

At breakfast, he and Alice were alone. He said: 'What is it that makes you so afraid?'

'I don't know. What is it that makes you so brave?'

'I don't know.'

But back in her bedroom, combing her hair, she thought about it again. And decided it was imagination. Everyone said she was imaginative: her mum, her nan, her dad. Kat. Kat's mum. They said that she was able to picture things vividly, feel stuff. In particular she could always imagine the worst, what it would be like, the awfulness of it – and dwell on it. She suspected Robbie's mind didn't work like that.

At breakfast Robbie had talked about the ruins on the island. The moment he'd mentioned them she'd shuddered. But he'd been cheerful, matter-of-fact, and then excited as his plans had taken shape.

Tom the steward had told him that the ruins on the island were once buildings belonging to a monastic community; they were a rather strange lot of monks though. Monks, usually, were dedicated to the cause of peace. These weren't; these were fighting monks. Like the Knights Templars. Similar, but not so popular – and very secretive. And there'd been some dispute. The king's men had come – a king of a long time ago – and there'd been resistance, fighting. The monks lost of course, and any still alive had their feet cut off. And then they had been left there to rot.

The forest had long since reclaimed the road that once went to the lake – and the buildings had fallen down. Only ghosts and evil spirits lurked there now. Everyone was certain. No one wanted to go near the place. Everyone said it was cursed.

Robbie said, 'It's the perfect place to hide. Or to leave someone that you don't want found. Your dad could have gone there. He might even be there now. We'll have to go and look.'

'We being you and Tom?' said Alice hopefully.

'We being me and you,' said Robbie with a huge grin.

First she insisted on showing him the map. She'd found it among her dad's things. Well, what was left of them after the men who came searching for him had gone.

There'd been three of them – the men. They were rough, uncouth. Not the sort you'd expect would work for the Cardinal.

The men had looked at the map. They had unrolled it but then dropped it carelessly, apparently discarding it. It probably wasn't significant – except that she'd wondered if it might be. She knew very little about her dad's work but she couldn't imagine why her dad had it; there wasn't a name on it anywhere that she recognised.

However, there was a sea monster in the sea. Much like Robbie's sea monster. The one he'd drawn and then shown her just over a year ago.

'So you think I'd know about this because of drawings of sea monsters,' laughed Robbie.

'Why not! Don't laugh at me.' Her face had become furious. Robbie continued to grin.

'You're a very silly, clever person.'

She calmed, frowned. 'Why am I clever?'

'Because, as it happens, I know of the places on this map. I know where it is. And it might well be a clue. It's…'

He stopped. Alice had come suddenly close. Thrust her hand over his mouth. 'There's someone on the stairs,' she whispered. 'Someone's listening!'

They were in the top room of the tower. No one came to the tower much; its three rooms were the coldest and dampest in Alice's house and in recent times the lower ones had been mainly used for storing meat. But her father kept other things in the top room: a trunk of documents and tally sticks, miscellaneous bits of old armour, and weapons – several swords and daggers. Its south facing window was a splendid vantage point from which to view the manor's fields.

To get up to the room they'd had to ascend a narrow stone spiral staircase. Robbie waited for Alice to walk back over to it, to investigate the noise – or whatever she'd heard. It was, after all, her house – it was bound to be one of her servants on the stairs.

She didn't move, just stood white faced.

'Go on.'

She shook her head. 'No.'

'Fine.'

Robbie tiptoed over and edged onto the first step. Then the second. How stupid not to have picked up one of the smaller weapons, he thought. One of the daggers.

Robbie held his breath and realised he could hear someone below him breathing.

Then there was a head, a man's.

'What do you want?' said Robbie.

The head jerked up, showing a simpering face. 'Just to come up, master.'

'So come. What stopped you?'

'Shoe trouble.'

'Really?'

Robbie went back to the top room; the man followed.

'Matthew,' gasped Alice.

'Matthew?' echoed Robbie.

'One of the servants,' said Alice.

'Who'd better start explaining. Fast!' snarled Robbie.

The servant gave them a supercilious smile. He was a middle-aged man, taller than Robbie. He didn't seem at all cowed.

'I've come from your mother,' said Matthew, ignoring Robbie, his tone cool and sarcastic.

'And?'

'And I said to Lady Catherine, that if your young friend wants to go exploring and getting lost like the last time I'd better come too. To stop you doing anything too stupid.'

'And she said yes?'

'She agreed with me.'

'Don't be impertinent. What did Mummy, Lady Catherine, actually say?'

'I made my offer. She said nothing. Which means yes. To say nothing means yes. It's the law ain't it. Silence means acceptance. I knows the law.'

Robbie said, 'Well my law says we don't want you. So now go away.'

CHAPTER FIVE

THE ISLAND

The map went with them in a satchel together with some food and drink. 'I don't trust Matthew,' said Robbie. 'We don't want him looking at it.'

'You haven't explained why it matters.'

'I'm not certain that it does. But I am certain that we need to get going while Matthew doesn't seem to be around.'

'You think he might try to stop us?'

'I think he might try to follow us.'

A long dagger from the room in the tower went with them too. When they reached the edge of the forest Robbie put it in his hand and said, 'Explorers need to prepare for the unexpected, because you just don't know what's out there.'

'No monkeys, I think. No parrots. No heat greater than our hottest summer.'

'No?' Robbie frowned, laid a hand on her arm. 'The last time I was here you didn't know what a parrot was.'

'Well I've been finding out. I even know about your Columbus and Cabot.'

'What do you know?'

'One found the north of it and one found the south of it.'

'Of what?'

'Somewhere called the New World.'

When they reached the place where the forest path met the stream, Robbie said, 'The trees are so thick here we could be in a jungle. Butterflies as big as your head fill the air, snakes as thick as your leg slither over the ground. There's one!' Robbie lunged with the knife at a low snake-like branch.

'Don't!' Alice covered her face with her hands.

'It's just pretend.'

'I don't want to.'

'You can't be scared of a branch.'

'It's just that when I pretend, it becomes real.'

'That's good. I'll be Columbus. Follow me.'

Following Columbus didn't help. Not even when Robbie said things like, 'Someday he'll be so famous there will probably be a rhyme about the year. So that no one forgets it. In 1492 Columbus sailed the ocean blue. Or something.'

'They won't. They won't care. Who'd care about poxy jungles!'

'Everyone.'

'No.'

She hated being in the stream. She was a year older but it made no difference. The water was flowing faster than she remembered it, plants growing at its edges moved forcefully against her legs. She kept thinking of bug-like things that might be swimming close. And eels. The thought of an eel slopping into her legs, or of stepping on one, made her feel sick. And when Robbie started talking about crabs, every large stone she glimpsed became one.

Robbie was enjoying it – clearly. The water was cold but the air was warm; sunlight stabbed down through the trees, the light was green and yellow. Sometimes Robbie stopped, faced her, and told her about fantastical creatures they might find: unicorns, great fire dragons whose brains were composed of precious stones, savage natives with faces in their stomachs, tribes with four elongated eyes in their foreheads, men and women who languidly fed upon nothing but honeysuckle dried in smoke....

'Keep your eyes open. Look out for them,' he said.

She wouldn't, and told him to shut up.

He laughed and splashed onwards.

Her skirt was soaked by the time they reached the lake. She'd tried to hitch it up, hold it up, but she'd stumbled and dropped a shoe. Now that they'd stopped moving, she'd started shivering violently.

They both stared at the island.

It seemed to be staring back. The window in the ruins of the chapel-tower part seemed to trap and blink sunlight like a malevolent eye.

'We need to get across to it,' said Robbie, 'but how?'

'Well you're the explorer.'

'Can you swim?'

'No. Can you?'

'Not really.'

'I don't know anyone who swims.'

'It would be useful though.'

'Do you think so?' She couldn't think why. Unless you were on a boat or a ship which was sinking. But not many people went on boats. 'Anyway, I don't see anyone over there. There's no one there. We don't need to go.'

'We ought to be sure.'

'Because it's part of your game?'

'No. Because we need to be sure. We have to eliminate it from the list of places we need to investigate.'

'You've got a list?'

'A long one.'

He didn't have a list. He'd made that up: to stiffen her resolve and to suggest that he was doing more than just planning on the hoof. Right now, though, his only plan was to get across to the island. He had to work out a way to get there; he had to ensure that Alice would come too.

He didn't think it was a place he'd want to visit alone.

There was at least a hundred yards of water to cross. It seemed very still water; very deep, although perhaps it wasn't.

He handed the satchel to Alice, removed as much of his clothing as seemed decent and waded out. A lake was a new experience. He'd messed around in the breaking waves at the edge of the sea, but he'd never wandered in so far that the water came over his shoulders. Very few ever did.

After the first shock of the cold, the sensation was extraordinarily pleasurable – until the water lapped just under his chin. Which it did quite quickly, far too quickly, just ten or so paces in. Then he had to turn back – and then he remembered rafts.

Two or three big logs or branches fixed together would suffice, he thought. It would only take two or three. He wasn't sure how he'd fix them. But he waded back fast, excited, energised.

Almost at the shore, he tripped and fell. All of him went under. He stood up muddy, panicked and furious.

There was intense pain in his foot too. Whatever had tripped him had been very solid. He felt for it, found a length of chain as thick as a viper, and hauled on it. The lake's bottom disturbed: mud, bubbles and something big as a bathtub began to surface. For an awful moment Robbie supposed it to be some dangerous aquatic beast. It wasn't. It was a small boat. An intentionally sunk boat. A small punt-like one.

There were big stones in its bottom. They had to lift them out. Alice didn't want to wade far into the water. Robbie did most of it.

Though Alice, standing among reeds as tall as she, helped drag the boat in. As the water, mud and slime poured out she was filled with a new dread.

'Who'd want to hide it?' she said. 'Why would they bother?'

'Isn't it obvious?'

'I hate it when people do that.'

'What?'

'Make it clear that they know the answer but don't say. Just to make a person feel small. It's hateful. Mean. But then you are, aren't you.'

'Mean enough to come fifty miles to help you?'

'So help.'

Robbie, just for a moment, thought he would help by slapping her. But then he didn't, and was troubled because he wasn't used to bending to criticism; usually when people threw censure at him, the schoolmaster mainly, his friends very rarely, his parents just sometimes, he took little notice. So he was puzzled, really puzzled, that it seemed to matter to him right now that Alice was cross.

But it did.

He made some effort to be kinder. He said, 'Sorry,' gently. Then he said, 'I don't really know, but obviously someone has something to hide. And secrets usually imply wrongdoing. So someone somewhere is guilty of something. We need to find out what.'

There wasn't a paddle with the boat. But the water's surface looked calm; there was very little wind.

They used their hands. And some bits of tree bark.

They had to work hard to get the rhythm right: they had to stretch forward together, dig their hands deep, pull the water back with a similar thrust. Robbie kept pulling back harder than Alice. Every time he did, the boat skewed sideways; sometimes it almost turned a circle. Robbie had to adjust to Alice's strength. Getting across took an agonisingly long time.

Alice whimpered for almost the whole way; she had never been on water in a boat; she expected to be swirled away at any moment by some sinister current. The moment they reached the island's reed beds she jumped out, splashing noisily through the knee high water, spooking wildfowl, careless of stealth. More amused than annoyed, Robbie waded after her, dragging the boat. When he caught up, she was sitting on a fallen tree branch at the shore's edge her face turned from him, hugging her knees to her chest.

He said, 'Told you I'd get you here. It's time you learned to trust me.'

She turned slowly and looked accusingly at him. Her face was ash-white. 'What are we to do if we meet the ghosts of the monks?' she said humourlessly. 'Stab them with your dagger?'

'Ghosts only inhabit the dark.'

'Do you have any idea what time it is?'

'I think a little after midday.'

'Whatever happens we've got to be away from here and out of the forest before sunset.'

'We will. One way or another this shouldn't take long. There's really not much left standing to explore.'

Only the chapel walls and its tower had been built solely of stone. Some walls of the other buildings had been, but there had also been wood, wattle, daub and thatch. All the roofs had gone. Plants had invaded huge areas. Wood had rotted and fallen. But the chapel stood proud.

Robbie went straight to it. It was like a small church; a heavy oak door still barred its front entrance; Robbie had to put his shoulder to it and shove.

It wasn't just the rusty hinges, but there was also debris piled behind the door.

'I don't think we should go in,' said Alice, 'if things have fallen down.'

'So you stay here and wait.'

'No!' Her face creased in panic. 'It's just that we shouldn't be alone. Not here.'

'So come on then.'

Robbie negotiated the rubble. She followed, slipping and scrabbling much more, but keeping up. She was desperate to keep up. She didn't want him to get more than a yard ahead.

But it wasn't so bad, she decided – when finally daring to lift her eyes from Robbie's back and look around. There was lots of sunlight, hardly any roof, and lots of glassless windows, which made it less scary.

There was an odd, unpleasant smell, though – somewhere between musty parchment and rotting apples.

Really quite odd.

Robbie walked down the nave to the south transept. Alice followed. In the transept, the roof was still largely intact; patches of limewashed plaster covered some parts of the walls – though where it didn't, the bare stone surface was dust grey; mossy stuff grew from its cracks and damp. In the room's middle, someone had arranged stones into a circle to contain a fire.

'Someone's been here,' said Robbie, poking at the charred sticks. 'Not so very long ago.'

'Ghosts don't light fires!'

Alice stared searchingly at Robbie; Robbie's eyes looked back bright with excitement. She just didn't understand why he wasn't frightened, but she clenched her hands into fists and resolved to be braver.

'There's a door. Just there,' whispered Alice, suddenly seeing it.

'Probably into the sacristy.'

'I'll look.' Alice stepped towards the door.

'Wait.'

'Why?'

'Just wait.'

The horrid smell seemed stronger here. And suddenly Robbie had remembered – identified it. He was almost certain.

He checked his grip on the dagger and stepped cautiously towards the sacristy door. The smell was the stench a dead body makes – if it hasn't found the way to its grave.

In Bristol, as in towns everywhere, people died young due to illness and accidents, fights and murder – mainly illness. Death was something you couldn't ignore.

Not many made it past forty.

Robbie had seen corpses but he'd seen nothing like what he found now.

In the sacristy, there was a table and a chair. On the chair was a headless body. On the table was the head.

Robbie recognised the head. And turned fast. To stop Alice from seeing.

But it was too late.

Alice was at his shoulder, mouth open as if to scream. No sound came out, though. No sound until Robbie led her right out of the building. Then she began to shake. 'That's my daddy,' she said.

CHAPTER SIX

FISH GIRL

Until they reached the boat Alice said nothing more. She followed Robbie, maintained his brisk pace, kept so close he felt her rattled breath on his neck. At the boat, in a voice little more than a croak, Alice said, 'I'm not crying? Why not? I should be. I should be crying!'

'You're in shock. It doesn't really seem real. Not yet.'

'Why are we leaving – him?'

'We've got to tell someone.'

'Who?'

Robbie wasn't sure. As he began to paddle, pushing the tree bark deep, trying to make speed, he attempted to give order to his thinking. Whoever had done it, presumably, was fairly certain that the body wouldn't be found for a long time. Whoever had done it, had known it was a place people avoided like the plague. That person, or persons, must have had reason to kill. And, probably, have the resolve to do it again...

Might think nothing of killing them...

Aghast, Robbie thought: was there anyone he shouldn't tell? For if he judged it wrong, he might tell the enemy.

The boat was refusing to go straight. Alice wasn't helping. She was hardly paddling at all. Mostly, her hands just trailed in the water – as if they didn't belong to her.

Frustrated, Robbie stopped paddling, sat up, tried to gauge how far they had still to go. He searched for the place where the stream met the lake. He expected to see it easily, but wherever the lake stopped the forest's trees tangled together and the lowering sun dazzled off the water's top. The stream had to be there, but probably, he decided, you wouldn't be able to see it until you came really close. He bent low to resume paddling, but made one further glance in the direction where he thought the stream must be. He gasped. There was a man, standing there, at the water's edge. Matthew – Alice's servant. Then two other men. Men he didn't recognise.

Matthew raised his arm and waved.

'I never imagined I'd be pleased to see him, but I am,' said Robbie. 'Who's that with him? Alice?'

'Don't know. Don't care.'

'Help me paddle.'

'Yes.'

Just for a moment, as Alice began to help, the boat went better, moved straighter. Then, suddenly, it went down at the stern – as if an anchor had been dropped off it. The boat dragged back. The stern sank.

Alice and Robbie turned together. They saw a hand – a surprisingly brown hand – hanging onto the back of the boat.

Then they saw a mop of black wet hair and a girl's face coming up. Surfacing. A face of red-brown skin, with a snub nose. With busy, anxious eyes.

A face quite unlike any Robbie or Alice had ever seen before.

'Bad men,' said the girl.

Robbie thought the girl was about Alice's age. Unlike Alice, she could swim. She was swimming now, surprisingly fast, round and round the boat. But with each circuit, she moved a little further out from them, a little further off.

Bad men?

'But its Matthew,' said Alice beseechingly.

'And this morning we didn't trust him, did we,' said Robbie.

'But should we trust this… this creature? It's either enchanted or knows enchantment.'

'Follow,' said the girl.

'What in God's name are you?' demanded Robbie.

'Follow.'

Suddenly, Alice attempted to stand. Swaying, almost falling, she tried to position herself between Robbie and where the girl was. The boat rocked alarmingly; water slopped in. Robbie shoved Alice back. Pulled her down. 'Stay sat. Stupid!'

Alice turned on him. Imploring. She said, 'But you mustn't look.'

'Why not?'

'I don't think she's wearing any clothes. You mustn't.'

Her pleading eyes wobbled him. And yet… Robbie looked out beyond Alice. Strained to see. It was difficult to be certain. The girl kept moving; the water constantly rippled around and over her. But then he glimpsed buttocks. Flesh. His heartbeat lurched.

Her body disappeared. All of her went under. Out of his sight. When she reappeared she was much further away; closer to the island. He could see only her head; the tops of her arms. She was treading water...

'Follow, now!'

She'd shouted it: shrill, her tone, desperate. And then she was off again – swimming away from them.

Robbie's eyes followed – as if they were glued to her. Captivated – utterly: by the graceful, fish-like ease of her swimming; the apparent nakedness.

'Robbie!' Alice was shouting again, tugging at his arm. Reluctantly, he tore his gaze away, glanced back at Matthew. In the last few minutes the wind had strengthened; it was drifting them in the servant's direction. Now they were only fifty yards from him – and from the shore. Less. Matthew was shouting that they must hurry. Go faster. It was clear he was agitated. Fearful.

'You have to help me paddle,' Robbie said to Alice. 'We need to turn the boat around.'

She looked at him coldly. 'Surely you're not going to follow that? Her?'

'Why not?'

'Because you always act first and think second. You haven't yet thought.'

'And you're always too scared ever to act.'

Alice sucked in her cheeks. 'At least I imagine the consequences.'

'This really isn't the moment for a dissection of your mind.'

'Is that so! Really? In front of us is my servant Matthew. Behind us is an island of evil spirits that killed Daddy. What's to dissect?'

'I don't think evil spirits killed your father. And I say, we should follow the girl.'

'A girl that's a fish?'

'Just turn off your brain and paddle.'

The girl reached the island many minutes before they did. By the time they were back in the reed beds she was dressed.

They stayed, feet in mud and water, next to the boat. The girl stood on the land, very still, several yards from them, with her arms folded as if considering. There was a resolute hardness: in her face; in her manner.

Clearly she wasn't a fish. But the clothes she wore were unusual, made from some kind of animal. Deer most probably, Robbie thought.

'You'd think she'd been dipped in honey,' whispered Alice breathlessly at his elbow.

'Don't be daft.'

'I'm not. Just look at her. Those brown eyes could easily be liquid-honey. And her hair's glossy, as if honey's been brushed into it. Her skin's honey-brown – her face is weirdly pretty. Don't you think she's pretty? Do you know what I think? I think she might be one of those people from far away lands that you said about. The ones that only feed on honeysuckles dried in … What was it?'

'Dried in smoke?'

'Yes.'

'She couldn't be.'

'Why not? It's what you said. And now you must find out what she knows about my... About my...' Alice swallowed hard and sucked in breath to steady herself. She crooked a finger imperiously at the girl. 'Hey, you, Honey, come here.'

The girl didn't move.

'I think she's expecting us to go to her,' said Robbie. 'Come on.'

'Or maybe she doesn't really speak English.'

'English, I speak, very well,' said the girl fiercely.

CHAPTER SEVEN

BRIGHT-AS-FLOWERS

As it turned out her English really wasn't very good. But she said they must trust her. That they would, once she explained. That they must let her explain.

They stayed on a little shingly beach while she said this. Alice didn't want to go near the buildings. Robbie wanted to keep watch on Matthew – and his companions.

Whoever they were!

'Bad men,' said the girl, again – but didn't elaborate.

But she came and stood closer. And after some moments of contemplation, searching faces, they sat down together, and Alice dug fingers into the sand and mud and shingle, lifting stuff up, letting stuff fall, examining it with such intensity that it was as if it were all that mattered – Robbie thought. The girl, also, watched Alice, silently, thoughtfully. Robbie and the girl shared a smile. The sun drifted lower. Matthew gave up his hostile shouting – and when sound became only birds, the breeze stirring trees, the water lapping, the girl – in stammering, broken English – began to feel her way into her story: told them that she was Bright-as-flowers, aged thirteen, come from a place people such as Robbie called the New World. That she'd been sent by her father to meet with England's King.

'Bright-as-flowers! What a mouthful,' said Alice. 'Honey's so much better.'

An exploring, enterprising ship had come to her lands from Bristol, hoping to trade wool and cloth. At first, her people had believed the Bristol sailors to be gods; they soon realized they weren't. But her people liked the cloth and her father, chief of her people, thought he would send her and another man to Bristol to meet with the Bristol chief, and then the English King. Most of this agreement had been through sign language – there had been a lot of guesswork.

She hadn't wanted to journey across an ocean, but her father had said she must – and the Bristol men had been kind, and she didn't think she'd be away very long. But the ship's journey had taken two moons. And off the coast of Cornwall, just past the Lizard, the ship had foundered, striking rocks, sinking in moments. Three sailors, only, survived; her companion hadn't.

Bright-as-flowers had swum straight to the shore. She'd learnt to swim at an early age. Beavers had been some of her earliest friends.

'What was the ship's captain's name?' asked Robbie.

'Captain Fletcher,' said Bright-as-flowers.

'Fletcher? He'd been to my house. Was involved in business

with my father. My father told me that Fletcher's ship sank. The Swan wasn't it? Odd that he didn't mention a princess…'

She'd been taken to London – eventually. To Henry VIII's court; the Tudor king there in his prime: twenty-nine years old, successful in war, popular at home. The only dark cloud in his world was that he didn't as yet have a son. His wife, Katherine of Aragon, once a most beautiful Spanish princess, had seen most of her babies die. One, a girl, Mary, lived, but there wasn't a surviving son. Not yet.

Unexpectedly, Queen Katherine was, apparently, pregnant with child when Bright-as-flowers went to be presented. Nevertheless, Queen Katherine, like most of the court-people, was unable to contain her amazement and excitement at meeting a princess from such far away lands; lands discovered by John Cabot for King Henry's father, just twenty or so years before.

Smiling, a wide, joyous smile, the queen leaned forward in her chair and beckoned Bright-as-flowers forward. She stroked Bright-as-flowers' cheek; made some pithy remark about Bright-as-flowers' odd nose.

King Henry laughed. The courtiers laughed. Then, suddenly, the queen clutched her belly and shrieked.

In great pain. Fear stark in her face.

She was ushered quickly away.

Before the day was over, Bright-as-flowers had been told that Queen Katherine's child, the one growing inside her these last four months, had died. She was told it accusingly, angrily, by several of King Henry's men; they gathered around her, handled her roughly, pushed her about. She, Bright-as-flowers, had done it, they said. Must have. By magic. Witchcraft magic. She was a devil, spawned of a devil. It was why the ship had sunk; she had caused it to sink. Witches raised storms and sank ships – everyone knew it to be so.

You had only to look at her to see that she wasn't fully human...

Then, she'd been carted off to a damp, cold, slit-windowed room in a London castle – in a tower. Examined, prodded about, hurt.

Then rescued.

By the man now dead. Beheaded. In the chapel. The chapel just there...

'But that's my daddy,' sobbed Alice.

~

Alice's father first met Bright-as-flowers when she'd arrived in London. He'd been involved with the group of men who'd escorted her to the palace. She and he hadn't actually spoken until the rescue. Until after he flung open her prison's door.

Hit hard, a man, one of the jailors, crumpled backwards into Bright-as-flowers' cell. He sprawled at her feet. Alice's father, Sir Lionel, stepping into the room, gave a grunt of satisfaction, kicked the man's head, then pulled Bright-as-flowers to the door and hurried her along the low ceilinged, twisting passage that led to the stairs. At the stairs they paused.

'You must keep very quiet,' hissed Sir Lionel. 'Or we'll both be dead.'

Mouth dry, she said nothing.

They crept down. The steps were spiralled, narrow. Sir Lionel led. At the stair's bottom, a small room. A guard sat at a table, his back to them.

They could have tried to creep past, but Sir Lionel decided not to take the chance of discovery. He lunged forward, and with a long knife slit the man's throat as he turned. The man tried to scream, but all that came out was blood.

'Now. Quickly,' Sir Lionel said.

They crossed the room, the bloodied knife in Sir Lionel's right hand, Bright-as-flowers' hand in his left. To another door – a strong beam of April sunlight stabbing through it, as if beckoning.

But this way out was suddenly blocked: a man's shadow, then the man coming in seeing the knifed man.

The man coming in shouted his anger. He was probably a guard. He had a weapon.

Sir Lionel rushed at him. Taking him by surprise; before he could gather his wits. He managed a second shout though. As he went down – a piercing shriek for help as Sir Lionel's knife plunged into his abdomen.

Now there would be other men.

Sir Lionel took in a deep breath and collected some composure. He gave Bright-as-flowers a wink of encouragement, said, 'Try not to look frightened. Or we'll not get out,' and walked slowly out into the courtyard.

To the first man who came running over, Sir Lionel said authoritatively, 'Be quick, damn you! Men have broken in. Are trying to free prisoners. Hurry.' And he pointed in the direction of the room from which he had just exited. The man rushed off. And others, arriving, followed. The moment they had gone, Sir Lionel, gripping Bright-as-flowers' arm, dragging her along, ran to the stables. His horse was saddled and ready. Bright-as-flowers eyed it dubiously and backed away. She had never seen a horse until her arrival in England. She had never sat on one.

'It don't bite, girl,' Sir Lionel said.

She gave him a fierce look. 'I'm not girl. I'm Bright-as-flowers.'

'And you're making my horse nervous.'

The horse was jerking its head. Snorting. Sir Lionel stroked its nose, made Bright-as-flowers pat its head. Then swept her up onto the saddle and, using the stirrup, climbed up behind her. He made her put her arms behind her back so that her hands could grasp his belt. A dig with his heels into the horse's flank got it moving. The moment they were into the courtyard he kicked it harder, urging speed, heading for the arch of the gatehouse. The gatehouse's sentry stepped out to block their way but, realizing the horse was almost into a gallop, changed his mind, stepped aside.

Once out in the street, the horse had to be reined in. There were too many people – and ox-carts and animals: pigs, some herded sheep. The streets were no wider than the carts; houses and shop fronts squeezed into every available space. But the bustle there, the animated jostling and people-movement, would slow pursuers too. Sir Lionel took care to move down the streets as unobtrusively as possible, trying to cause no alarm, hoping that no one would remark on his passing. Only once he was over London Bridge did he seek to go faster. Though he had to be careful not to overtire the horse.

It took three days to reach Sir Lionel's home. As they travelled, he didn't try very hard to put Bright-as-flowers at her ease and she didn't try to be anything other than aloof –determined to make it quite clear that she knew herself to be Sir Lionel's superior.

He repeated often, 'It's for the best girl.' Kept saying it…

She wouldn't meet his eye; she looked into the middle distance – fought back her tears.

The best moments for Bright-as-flowers were when the track left the more open cleared land around the villages and plunged down into the deep oak forests – when the clop of the horse's hooves and the creak of reins and saddle were the main noise; plus bird-sounds: their songs and fluttering and flight – and a sometimes glimpse of deer. But best of all, the trees' silence that spoke. As a deer could sometimes too. And other creatures: the almost-sound that Bright-as-flowers was attuned to hear.

The trees' buds were unfolding; woodland plants were with flower. With the forest around her she felt heaps better. Brave.

The weather became malevolent before they reached Sir Lionel's house. High wind, bitingly cold, sleet – some stuff almost snow. Darkness came early, but Sir Lionel welcomed that; he wanted to arrive unseen, leave the horse, leave a message for his wife and move on. Too dangerous to stay at the house; his enemies mightn't be far behind.

Not far.

Seven days earlier he'd reconnoitered the ruins of the monastery on the lake's island. And arranged for supplies: food mainly; a boat with paddles – getting all of it put there by his most trusted servant, John; the stable's man. Sworn to secrecy.

The night of his return he left his horse with John.

But Sir Lionel's enemies, aided by Matthew, had found him; killed him. They'd paid Bright-as-flowers no attention while they did it. They didn't know she could swim.

'But why did he rescue you?' said Alice, plaintively.
    'He was good man,' said Bright-as-flowers.
    'There must be more to it than that,' Robbie said, and he reached for Alice's hand, to bring comfort, clasp it tight.
    She snatched her hand away.

CHAPTER EIGHT

DEER PATHS

As darkness began to close in, they saw that Matthew – or the men with him – had managed to light a fire at the shore's edge.

Robbie and Alice watched its glow with desperate, intense longing. At their backs the darkness pushed, pressed like something alive; and Alice particularly imagined the most awful things lurking there – and in a quivering gasp-voice kept saying so.

'Just try to fill your mind with thoughts of nice things,' urged Robbie. 'Favourite things.'

'Don't patronize me. In fact, just shut up!'

Alice shouted the last bit – the 'shut up' – hysterically. As she did so, Robbie heard Bright-as-flowers, sitting next to him, click her tongue disapprovingly.

At least the men had given up their shouting, Robbie thought. Given up urging them to climb into the boat and paddle back. And possibly, probably the men were not all of them there now; only two silhouettes could be made out close to the fire. One gone for help, presumably. To summon more people. Or a boat! It had to be the case that neither Matthew nor his cronies could swim well enough to get across. Bright-as-flowers – Honey (Alice kept insisting on 'Honey') – scoffed at the fact that most English people seemed to not be able to swim.

Honey, of course, swam like a fish – but she preferred, she said, comparison to beavers. When she was a young child, beavers had been friends, she said. And, interestingly, the liquid-brown of her darting eyes brought easily to Robbie's thoughts, eyes of rodents. Honey's had that same bright, flickering alertness. Indeed, there was something very animal-like about her; particularly her watchfulness – and the sudden moments when she seemed to tense, freeze, as if bringing all her senses into play; those were animal-like too.

Contrastingly, there was also, he thought, a strange nobility inhabiting her. An aloof poise; a snappish decisiveness. If she were an animal she'd be more cat than rat.

Robbie said, 'We must decide what to do, make a plan,' and directed his words more towards the shadowy shape of Honey than Alice.

Alice answered first, however. A stifled sob. And: 'The only plan I want is to go home.'

'Well that can't happen, can it! We have to keep Honey safe. Finish what your father started.'

'They'll track us down. Wherever we go. We might as well give up now. Give them what they want.'

'Give them Honey!'

'They won't hurt her.'

'Crap!'

He peered at Alice, tried to discern her expression – but it was too dark. Robbie hoped she looked ashamed. He was ashamed of her. But he didn't want to be cross with her – swear at her; what with her father's appalling death … 'Look, sorry,' he said, forcing it out.

She didn't reply.

Robbie dragged his thoughts back to planning. Destination? The: where to go?

Since evening arrived he'd been desperately trying to make connections. Was there a connection between the map Alice had found and Honey? The map showed a part of the New World. So what did Alice's father have to do with the New World – the place some people had begun to call America? Why did Alice's father care enough about Honey to rescue her? Put his life on the line? His reputation? If it had been his own father involved, it would have made more sense. A little more sense.

Which made his father the obvious place to start. Didn't it?

Robbie said, 'We must get to my parent's house. Get to Bristol. Two days and a night – three at most. Three and we'd be there. He'd know what to do. My dad would know.'

Alice snorted. 'That's stupid. The men'd find us. It's obvious we'd try that. The Bristol road's obvious. They'd check that road.'

'We move fast. Keep ahead.'

'And they might have horses.'

'We…'

Honey stopped him. Stood in front of him, pressed a finger across his lips.

'Forest,' said Honey. 'We go. Deer paths. Way, I find. Isn't it.'

The decision was made. Two against one. Alice didn't like it – and for a time they had to put up with her glower because unexpectedly the clouds slid away from the moon.

They waited for the clouds to return. When they did, Honey tugged off her clothes and put them into the boat. Robbie tried not to watch but his eyes kept drifting. Honey was much the same height as Alice, but she was a little fleshier, with more obvious beginnings of a woman's shape: waist, hips, breast bumps – bumps he couldn't properly see. And wouldn't now, unless moonlight returned.

'Robbie! Robbie get in,' said Alice crossly.

'Shush! No speak,' growled Honey.

Alice had scrambled into the boat. She lay along one side; Robbie joined her and, on the side opposite, did the same. She cringed, held breath. It was part of the plan: that they would lie flat, keep low – but she'd expected him to face away from her. He hadn't. And because even with legs bent up they filled the boat's length, their noses suddenly touched. She shuddered, her held breath shot out. She screwed her head away from him.

Honey pushed the boat out from the sedge, and slid down into the ink-black water. With her hands holding the stern, she began to swim. Her legs kicked the propulsion. She took care to keep her legs beneath the water's surface – not to splash, make noise.

The wind was making some; and there came out from the forest two sharp night-animal yelps – as if the one made had been answered. But mostly it was unnaturally quiet; so quiet that soon Alice could hear Honey's teeth chattering with cold – and when thinking about the water's cold and its appalling black depths, the closeness of Robbie's face, his breath on her cheek, ceased to matter.

Honey kept swimming: maintaining rhythm, focus, pushing the boat, making for the shoreline furthest from Matthew. Getting there. But, when they had almost reached it, were just ten or so yards off, strong moonlight returned and the water around the boat puckered up silver. Alice's eyes, still just inches from Robbie's, became luminous with it – enough for him to see her widening fear.

Trying to ease things, he whispered, 'It's all right. We want the clouds gone now. We'll need to be able to see the North Star.'

Her eyes narrowed, glared accusingly. 'Honey said we weren't to speak. In the boat.'

'And the sun tomorrow,' he added, more loudly, suddenly wanting to annoy her.

'Honey said to keep quiet. Honey said!'

'To keep west. Pole Star and sun. You see I know these things.'

'And I know: not a sound until the forest. Rubbish leader you're making.'

'Better than you would.'

'And your breath smells.'

They didn't go straight into the forest; they dragged the boat out of the water, hid it as best they could, and became acutely awkward, pointedly averting their gaze while Honey dressed. Then Honey led them along the lake's edge for several minutes. They slithered, sloshed through reed beds and mud. Suddenly, for no reason that was obvious to Alice or Robbie,

Honey ducked into the tangled, seemingly impenetrable undergrowth beneath a clump of alders.

They exchanged a glance and followed warily – but it was a track of sorts, a route presumably that deer made; they had to keep single file and duck low.

It was slow going; hard work: tripping, stumbling. The ground beneath their feet was so hard to see that each step in the darkness was like a step into a puddle of soot; roots and plant growth struck at them, clutched, scratched; their lashed legs ached. Alice muttered, shrieked sometimes, cursed.

Honey had the least trouble; she seemed to have an instinct for the path's course – and the best way to place her feet. But when Robbie and Alice paused for breath, to take stock, complain, Honey said she hated the darkness every bit as much as they did. Honey said that in her country, dark was the time when everyone went to the longhouse. That it was the time when all of her people would crowd close to the longhouse's central fire, get cosy beneath blankets – absorb tobacco and a story before sleep.

Honey wished she hadn't told them. When they started off again, try as she might, she couldn't stop thinking about nights in the longhouse. Night story-time was treasured. The stories – squints of remembrance, adventure, wisdom – most old as time, entertained, informed, connected, soothed. In her mind's eye now, there arrived one about the sky people whose anger was so fierce their hair would turn to hissing snakes. Extraordinary anger that once melted the moon... And in that one – one of her favourites – the moon was saved only because it landed on a turtle's back...

72

The time when the owl hunts, the wolf hunts, when the wind puffs beneath constellations of stars, is the time for stories, not for walking in the forest dark – she tried to say.

But the remembering was making her dreadfully homesick – desperately sad. And she had to keep that hidden from Robbie – and the whiny girl.

She had to be her father's daughter.

He wouldn't expect her to cry.

Fighting back tears, Honey suddenly stopped walking and bent low, burrowed into a spacious, suitable for night-sleep, bush-growth. On her knees she began to scoop and pile leaf litter to make a sidewall. The tears' nearness thwarted her attempts to explain to Robbie and Alice what she wanted them to do. Angrily, she worked on; meekly they waited. They heard her movements but saw little; the bush-space was black as Newcastle coal.

When all, finally, was ready, she managed, 'With the sun again we go. Now is the sleep, isn't it.' And curled tight into a cat-like ball.

CHAPTER NINE

―◆―

SEED BABIES

Birdsong woke them – a cacophony of it just over their heads. They jerked awake, surprised, and in Alice and Robbie's case embarrassed; in sleep they had curled together for warmth – were entwined.

But it was as well that they woke up warm; the early sunlight scarcely reached the forest's bottom; it would be a long time before the sun climbed high enough for shafts to cut through, reach them.

And until then there was a soaking mist. And greyness. And wet earth smell. But they had to press on. Put distance between themselves and Matthew. Get to Bristol. First.

'Drink, eat, not yet. Isn't it,' said Honey. 'We go.' She ushered Alice behind a tree to pee, wiped Alice's hands with moss, then led off; her steps remarkably deft – deer-like, Robbie thought.

Which was appropriate: Robbie reckoned they were still on a track made by deer, though there was often very little of a track to see. He told this to Alice; and told himself that the track's difficulty was good training for a budding explorer;

that teaching his body to function on an empty stomach was especially useful. But he couldn't stifle a growing irritability; and when they came upon a muddy place pock-marked with hoofprints, though he was certain they were made by deer, he was too miserable to point them out, show Alice that he'd guessed right.

Beyond the hoof marks, making headway was even harder: briars, low branches, tangles of roots, dense patches of plants that often pricked – sometimes stung. Presumably, the deer weren't much slowed by such things; or the other animals that made use of it: wild boar, badger, foxes; Honey wasn't overly slowed either…

But not keeping up, now Robbie's irritability burst into frustration. He took up a long stick, slashed at the undergrowth, snarling, furious. Alice, just behind him, flinched and began to snivel. After an especially difficult stretch, mostly bent low, almost on their knees, Robbie said loudly, 'I think we're going to have to risk the road. Sooner or later. Probably sooner. This is too slow. Too meandering. And we've nothing to eat.'

'Changed your tune,' snapped Alice. 'Finally … Next, Honey will change hers; agree to give herself up. Help me go home.'

'No,' said Honey imperiously, turning, moving back towards them, her face set fierce, defiant. 'This is safe way – and way for food, isn't it. I later find food. You keep up. Try more.'

She swivelled round, set off again.

Robbie and Alice exchanged a look of disbelief. 'She who must be obeyed,' muttered Robbie. 'Much better name than Bright-as-flowers – or Honey.'

'You don't like Honey because I thought of it.'

'I don't like Honey because it isn't her name.'

'No it's because I thought of it.'

'No.'

'Yes.'

Exasperated, Robbie fell silent.

Following. Their feet squelched through the sodden plant layer; above them, tree branches creaked when they rubbed. Robbie remained silent. Sometimes Alice swore: villagers' expressions – incongruous from her lips, Robbie thought. But, though the expletives made him smile, he didn't respond, comment – and she directed nothing at him that forced reply.

Honey didn't seem to feel any need to make conversation; she just went stoically on.

The sun, finally, had risen: warmth enough to push the mist off. Sweat dribbles ran down Alice's back. Though sometimes she shivered, for birds kept up noise and their disturbed, alarmed fluttering startled her. But mostly, now, she was lost in thoughts about her father. And her mother. Flashes of how her mother would be when she found out. How she would be this very moment too – her daughter a day missing.

A whole day... and the life before she was finding hard to keep a hold on.

Unlike the moments the sacristy door opened.

Kept remembering. That.

But then, as if from nowhere: a new worry – and, in an instant, she forgot the sacristy, her father's dead face. Her mother's likely reaction.

For her cousin Kat, only girl relation of similar age, at Christmas last, had told her boys, when they stopped being boys, were able to do what she must have seen horses, dogs, pigs, cattle do: grow some usually hidden body part into a several inches long pole. And that this pole was hollow – like a reed. And that a baby, small as a flower seed, could pass down the pole and enter into a woman – if a bed and cuddles and sleep were shared. And what had brought all of this back now, she realised, was because when she and Robbie had woken, earlier, she had felt something like a pole pressed against her. And if it had – and she thought it had – might a baby have passed down it and into her?

Her heart thudded hard. Surely such a thing couldn't have happened? Surely not!

Robbie was just in front of her, bending, wriggling under a low branch. She watched carefully, her eyes followed his body's pivot forward, jerk, straightening up. As he walked on, she thought, she couldn't for the life of her imagine that a baby could in any way spring out of him.

No.

And… and, such a thing as the pole didn't have to be true anyway. Because: Kat liked to tease her. Apparently she was easy to tease. Even village children would try to. Even her father…

Suddenly, it seemed obvious that this was what it must be. A tease. She trembled with relief. And then remembered something even better. Kat had said that special noises, groans, like witches' incantations, needed to be made too. She didn't think that had happened. Was good-as-hellfire certain. So pole or not, a baby couldn't be in her.

Not today.

The panic ebbed. And, as the worry eased she quickened her step, stooped and straightened, ducked and bent-double with a growing energy, managed more settled breaths, caught up with Robbie.

Reassurance tingled down through her.

She told herself she was just twelve years old, that she had every reason not to know lots of grown up stuff. All that mattered right now, she decided, was finding the best way to convince Robbie to take her home.

And convince Honey.

She began to rehearse that argument in her head: turned and twisted it about – but thoughts of the tiny seed-babies wriggled back. What if, she thought, there really was this … this pole thing, and a baby seed had somehow managed to slip down the pole, but had not be able to enter her? What might have happened to it? What careless end? Where might it be?

All at once: an agony of sadness for the imagined helpless baby poured in – and overwhelmed her. It was the last straw: one too-terrible thing too many. She found herself whimpering, her eyes hot and hurting.

Now she didn't want to go on. Her legs wouldn't work properly – when their wobbling made her think of egg custard, she found herself thinking: it's another ridiculous something to have floating about in my head. Egg custard! Whatever's wrong with my head!

She sat abruptly down. The plants were still wet and damped her. She stood up. Robbie was out of sight. She stifled sobs, called his name. Waited. No response. She wasn't feeling any better, but she reminded herself that if she didn't keep going they might leave her behind. Honey had good as said it. And Robbie? He hadn't waited for her to catch up for ages.

She clenched her hands into fists and made herself move. And as she began to edge forward, lose some of the unsteadiness, she decided that she might make herself go faster if she brought to mind some favourite thing. Robbie, last night, had told her to do that, to settle her nerves. She'd thought it stupid. Told him it was stupid. Last night. But now...

She tried to picture being sat by the hall fire, staring into its red-eye glow. Always that was the place that brought her calm; surely, she thought, it was the place, now, to help her walk. She half closed her eyes, imagined watching the flame flick; recalled the way it slipped her into trance. Her safe feeling. The world's presence removed. Even Mummy's.

Even Mummy would tiptoe round her.

Except on Leper Day!

Or the days just before Robbie's first visit...

On one of those days, Mummy – she suddenly remembered – had indeed tried to talk to her about making babies. But she'd scarcely listened. Hadn't wanted to.

She wished, now, with all her heart that she had. She desperately needed to know.

She thought, when I get home it's something I will do. I will! Ask Mummy. Find out.

Unless...

It struck her that she mightn't have to wait that long, that she could ask Honey. Honey, she thought ruefully, was just the sort of girl who'd know about making babies. She just had to find bravery enough to ask Honey. About babies...

She stopped dead.

The sitting by the fire stuff hadn't worked. Nor had she caught Robbie up. But baby stuff had stormed back.

Why?

Then it came to her that perhaps some enchantment, some wicked spell had been magicked to assail her. She realised that her chest was tight, her heart racing, that for some time now a dull ache in her stomach had been sharpening.

All were, she knew, tell-tale signs.

The possibility was terrifyingly real.

That she was under a spell.

She cried, 'Holy Mother and the saint's preserve me,' to break it. Repeated, shouted, screeched: hoping to startle the spell's evil out of her.

She began to run.

She crashed through plants, tree branches – then her foot tangled with a bramble's trail. She tripped, fell heavily. Robbie, hearing her wailed shriek, rushed back.

He found her slumped on the ground, fiercely scratching lumps of caked mud from where her skirt covered her knees. She growled, 'You call this a deer path. I think it's a path made by elves, to temp humans. To follow to their... their...'

'Doom?'

'Yes, doom!'

He laughed. Her face dissolved into something his mum called a picture of misery.

CHAPTER TEN

THE HUNT

'I didn't mean to laugh. I didn't want to. It just came out.'

'If you didn't want it to, it wouldn't have, would it.'

'Whatever you say.'

They were sat side by side. Alice was hunched up, hugging tightly her knees to her chest. Robbie had placed himself next to her. His mum's phrase had nudged him; and an odd churn of his stomach had accompanied it. A nudge, then a jolt: reminding him that she would expect kindness – him to Alice. And be forgiving.

Robbie, dearheart, Dad and I expect you to follow the Christian pathway to the letter – she'd say.

So now, with the loose material of his sleeve, he tentatively began to wipe the tear marks and mud grime from Alice's face. She let him. Not obviously disturbed by it. Perhaps she wasn't noticing?

Nevertheless, encouraged, he tried to think of something else to please her. He lifted the satchel off his body. The food he'd put in it yesterday was as good as finished, but he rummaged hopefully. 'You just need some breakfast to cheer yourself up,' he said.

He brought things out. The map. The dagger…

Under a crease at the bottom, Robbie found a thumbnail size piece of bread. Several other crumbs too. Taking great care not to drop any, he placed them into Alice's hand, closing her hand into a fist to contain them. He put the leather drink bottle to her lips, gave her its last beer swig.

As she finished licking up the crumbs, he watched her face carefully. He hoped she might smile. Mime a thank you. She didn't. Instead she said, 'All this bad luck is because of the leper. Did God send the leper? Why?'

He looked at her in surprise. Furrowed his brow. Considered.

'If God did, perhaps it was a test.'

'A test?'

'When you saw the leper coming, what did you do?'

I ran.'

' Perhaps you shouldn't have?'

'Don't be silly. You…'

She broke off, looked behind her in alarm – as if mentioning the leper had brought him back. But it was Honey who was there, emerging with almost no sound, like magic, out of a thick mass of undergrowth behind them. She squatted down on her haunches, shrugged her shoulders quizzically.

Alice returned the look. Plaintively she said, 'Didn't you say you'd get us food? Didn't you? Well, where is it? I don't see any.'

Honey narrowed her eyes. 'Soon, isn't it.'

'Soon!'

'Yes.'

Alice's face screwed up scornfully. She muttered something about her father being dead. That they didn't care…

Honey shook her head – an annoyed, exasperated shake. Then her eyes settled on the dagger. All annoyance went; excitement replaced it.

'It's my father's,' said Alice, following Honey's gaze. 'Which means it's mine.'

Alice snatched the dagger up and dropped it back in the satchel. The map too. And pointedly handed the satchel back to Robbie.

'Mine,' she repeated.

Honey got up. Walked away. Off along the deer path. Extraordinary – Robbie thought – that she so easily could. Most of the time to him, and to Alice, it didn't look at all like a way – only Honey seemed able to see that it was.

Utterly extraordinary…

'You don't need to be so obviously hostile,' whispered Robbie.

'And you don't really know anything about her. For all we know she might have… have killed my father. You don't know.'

'I do.'

'You really don't.'

He was afraid she was going to start crying again. Her lips were trembling; she was sucking in breath. He pulled her to her feet. 'Come on. We mustn't let Honey get too far ahead of us.'

'We don't have to follow her.' She fixed on him a serious, penetrating stare. 'We don't!'

He tried to brush some of the dirt from her clothes. He said, gently, 'You look like something the cat dragged in.' It was another expression of his mum's.

He got her going. And walked just behind – to keep her moving: sometimes cajoling, sometimes little pushes and harder shoves. Honey kept getting away: disappearing from view and their hearing. They never felt certain she would eventually stop and wait – but at regular intervals she did: searching their faces with baffled eyes, frowning impatiently.

She was struggling to accept them – Robbie thought.

'She scares me,' Alice said. 'Why doesn't she scare you?'

Alice was still finding it hard not to think about the baby stuff. Mainly, when to broach it with Honey.

Whether to…?

It wasn't helping that every time she and Robbie caught up, Honey seemed less and less approachable. She began to think that even if she could find a moment alone with her, she wouldn't manage to raise it.

And not just because it was Honey. She always found it hard to cope with working up to asking an awkward question. Exposing her ignorance. Usually, just imagining the asking, the resultant embarrassment, caused sick-in-her-tummy apprehension – she'd put the doing of it off: sometimes there'd be days and days of that. Which was a big reason she was happiest in her own company – biggest one. You never knew how other people were going to respond.

Or what they would expect: of her, from her. Unpredictability in people was heart-crash worry…

The sun was high overhead: middle of the dayish. It had become very warm. Above the leaf canopy the sky they glimpsed was shiny blue. The trees they walked between grew close; sun shafts arrowed down – mostly they walked through shadowy air mottled by them.

They had been on steep hillside slopes for a long time: with always more going up than down. Now they were descending; the slope was steep; beneath their feet, the leaf mulch was drier; under it grit and stones moved; dirt dusted. Sometimes they slipped. They heard the murmur of water long before they saw it. A stream? A river?

Hearing the water's flow, Honey kept closer, began to walk their slower pace. Her face made smiles; slipped into expressions of eagerness. She began to explain that usually she didn't catch fish – but she would. For them. Today. She explained that her water-skills were gifts from the spirits, that the creatures of the water-world demanded respect – that usually, if she didn't have to, she didn't eat fish.

'Then what did you eat on the island? What kept you alive?' Robbie asked.

'Sir Lionel left food. For day and many. And when it all gone, I swim to forest and trap animal. I was meant to stay on island, many day. So I do. Safe there until...'

'Until what?'

'Until the good... how you say...?'

'People?'

' People, yes. Come for me.'

'Us!' said Alice.

Honey wrinkled her small nose. Her eyes sparkled. ' Fish, isn't it,' she laughed.

It wasn't quite a stream or a river. Something, Robbie said, in between. A striddle. He said it hoping Alice would laugh, but she was already sinking onto her knees, looking into the water. It was very clear, he could see pebbles at its bottom shiny as Bristol's cathedral glass. She's looking at her reflection, Robbie thought. Girls!

Honey seemed to be doing the same. He turned away disappointed – but then couldn't stop from looking back. For the sunlight was bouncing up from the water, catching one side of Honey's face, glistening her dark long hair, softening the severe fine-boned cheeks it framed, easing the fit of her snub nose. He kept looking – and was surprised to suddenly realize that she wasn't, like Alice, admiring her reflection; she was examining animal prints at the water's mud-edge.

'Fish no,' she said. 'Better idea I have. Isn't it.'

There was, Robbie saw, mischievous gleam in her brown eyes.

She led off across the stream. It deepened as they went: up to their waists as they reached the far bank. The cold of it, momentarily refreshing, made them shiver. And the bank's overhang was steep. It was hard to get up it. Honey stayed in the water, got hold of Alice's legs, heaved her out. Sticky white sap, from plants grabbed as she scrambled forward, covered Alice's hands. She wiped them clean on Robbie's doublet as they resumed walking. By the time he'd finished protesting, Honey was out of sight.

At a place where the track appeared to split, they caught up.

Honey was sitting cross-legged; waiting. She said, 'You wait. Here. Stay here.'

'Here?'

'Wait. No move.'

She jumped up, put a finger in her mouth, made it wet, held it up to check the wind's direction. Then she carefully positioned Alice and Robbie upwind of where the track split, about twenty paces from it.

'Knife,' Honey demanded.

'Don't,' Alice said.

'No, we should... must... trust.' Robbie took it out from the satchel, bowed ceremonially, and handed it over. 'It's not a knife. It's a dagger,' he said. 'A weapon for fighting, stabbing. A very, very good one.'

Honey, clearly, agreed. She held it in her neat brown hands, turned it expertly, ran her thumb down it feeling the sharpness – grinned.

'You stay. Not move. Not noise,' Honey said.

She went thirty paces forward of them, downwind from where the track diverged. There she pulled herself a little way up into a large, ancient oak, and edged out along a thick branch close to the ground, overhanging the track. She lay flat, gripping it with her legs. She'd put the dagger between her teeth as she climbed; now she transferred it to her right hand.

Waited.

In her head, she examined her plan. It was fraught with risk – but if it worked the reward would be great. She would, surely, harness the trust and respect of her companions; she was keen to glue Robbie's loyalty – she very much approved of his thrusting spirit. As for the girl: she was the kind of child her father, without a moments regret, would have sold to their neighbouring tribe as a slave. Unfortunately, she owed a debt to Sir Lionel. She had to keep his daughter safe.

And fed...

There were deer close by. She was certain; she'd sensed them. And the knife – dagger – fashioned as it was for stabbing, gave her a reasonable chance of killing one. If she could get it deep into the neck, not get trampled by flaying hooves...

It wasn't something she'd try without Sir Lionel's weapon.

Not that she ever had. There was nothing half as good in her own lands; her people had small amounts of copper, but that was all. Iron was unknown to her people.

The iron dagger gave her a good chance. Her agility and bravery would too. First though a deer had to come.

She had to wait.

Wait...

She closed her eyes, pressed down her thoughts until she could picture only tree stuff, pushed her body down tight to the branch bark, imagined the scuttling insect life beneath scuttling in her. The deer couldn't see her if she was the tree.

She opened her eyes. Kept still as frozen.

Deer were close. She could feel their closeness. But even so she might have to not move for a long time. Knew she mustn't: a hunter knew.

She had hunted and seen a deer killed before.

Once.

With her father.

Hunting hadn't been the intention. They'd been to the sea, to their world's edge, stood where the water spits foam-stain on the land. They'd marvelled at its gifts: sea shells and coloured stones; the smell and taste of its scent...

They'd gone there to choose shells for a necklace – a treat; she'd turned twelve summers, a moment to mark. On the return journey the keen wind, dazzling sea sun, shrill bird cries stayed alive in her head even when the forest closed tight. Even in the places where sunlight came only if leaves had fallen (it being their time to).

Deep, deeper into the forest: the air thick: because the wind was unwilling to venture there. Middle of the afternoon, but drops of dark and drips of night lingering.

She remembered.

And her father, Steady Hand, suddenly, abruptly stopping. Saying, 'Wolf'. Smelling it!

She remembered...

Bending to examine the ground: showing her father, Steady Hand, pad marks – there had been rain. And a telltale disturbance of leaves.

Not that a lone wolf was something to fear – but her father cautioned that she keep still. Crouch, wait.

Probably the deer, which suddenly arrived, had been flushed out by the wolf; probably the deer, fearing the wolf, overlooked the crouched figures. The arrow that Steady Hand set loose (after only a moments aim, and the uttering of ritual chant seeking forgiveness) overlooked nothing, flew straight and true, allowing its target no time for reflection.

There was no whoop of joy; respect had to be shown to all creatures – in life and in death. It's a very serious Steady Hand cutting open the belly with his flint knife, making the necessary present of entrails to the forest. The same knife cut and peeled back tree bark to make a rudimentary sled; this was a deer too fat, too heavy to carry.

Dragging the deer lost the day, but Steady Hand smiled many wide smiles. Killing the deer had been a response to the moment: the response of beings governed by snow-fall following leaf-fall, hunger following plenty, death following birth. The deer surrendered its life as it was meant to; taking it completed a pattern.

She remembered.

And pangs of homesickness ambushed her.

Now, there were tears in Honey's eyes. Tears: clouding sight and judgment. Tears: as the prey she was hoping for appeared. Suddenly there – a deer: small, female, killable. Coming fast, spooked by the scent of Robbie and Alice.

Too fast

Almost beneath Honey's branch in moments. She launched off, aimed to land on the deer, stun it, plunge the dagger in…

She missed. Just. A hoof lashed her nose as the deer sprinted clear.

As she stood up, copious blood dripped from her nose down her front.

CHAPTER ELEVEN

WINN

Sullen. Silent. Except when Alice muttered: about feeling faint, or starving – or having stomach ache, leg ache, feet ache. Robbie hadn't spoken for a while – and nothing at all cheerful for a long while. Honey led, but slowly, without enthusiasm, her breathing laboured and through her mouth. She was dizzy; she feared her nose was broken. She clutched the dagger.

She hadn't tried again. Robbie had thought she should. Because it had nearly worked. But she knew they might have to wait hours, days even, for another chance. Deer were creatures soaked in fear: the deer-fear of the escaped one lay blanket thick on the forest air.

She felt ridiculed. Humiliated...

What she'd attempted had been clumsy. She should have thought of something better. She would... She would...

Lost in her thoughts, Honey emerged into a clearing without any of the caution that breaking the forest's cover demanded. Into a small space from which trees had been felled. There were gnarled stumps. There was a ramshackle house: small, isolated, the forest surrounding it – wood-smoke from its open-shuttered window, a thatch roof that almost came down to the ground, as if wanting to hide it. There was a small patch of cultivated land, fenced to keep out deer, growing herbs, and food plants: skirret clumps, leeks; several rows of just sprouting beans.

There were chickens.

Honey made as if to stalk a large black one.

'No!' said Robbie.

Honey glared at him. Robbie wondered if she understood the concept of property. 'It's not ours to take. Not ours.'

'Whose though?' said Alice nervously.

'Probably a verderer's cottage.'

'Or a witch.'

Robbie's face fell. 'I hadn't thought of that.'

'Perhaps you should,' said a voice.

The voice came from a protruding clump of trees to the left of them. A voice: rasping, wheezy.

Alice and Robbie both turned towards it in dread.

And expected to see an old, shrivelled, malevolent hag.

What they saw made them gawp.

She wasn't old, but young – though older than they were; but not much. Except that she stooped as if old, hunched forward onto a walking stick. And moved towards them slowly, with much care.

She laughed at their obvious confusion. Then coughed; winced – in pain.

The coughing eased. 'And what law says a witch must be aged and ugly?' she said, sternly.

'None, I guess,' said Robbie, warily – staring hard, seeing a wisp of a girl: pale face, untidy straw-coloured hair. She looked so much younger than her voice suggested… 'Though a really clever witch might call up a disguise,' added Robbie.

She smiled. The smile made her younger still. But she seemed to be finding it hard to gather breath.

'It is claimed there are ways,' she managed eventually. 'Bathing in the blood of young virgins… works. With the right spell.'

She took a firm step towards Alice. Waggled the stick. Robbie reached into the satchel for the dagger – and remembered that Honey still had it.

Honey was paying the stranger little attention. She was clearly not perturbed by her. She was watching a hen scratching the ground: grubbing.

Robbie tried to catch Honey's eye, but she was looking at the hen too keenly – keeping very still.

Unlike Alice. Alice was trembling – wild eyed.

The witch-girl stepped right up to Alice, put out a hand, lifted Alice's chin.

'We only want some food,' cried Alice. My father's dead. Mur… Ow!'

Robbie had taken hold of the upper part of her nearest arm; now he was squeezing it, making it pinched. Alice tore her arm away from him. Anger flashed in her face.

'Why not! Why can't I tell her? She might help.'

'Because, we don't know who she is.'

The witch-girl said thoughtfully, 'Come into my house then. Let me explain.'

The house inside was dark: the shafts of light coming from the open door and the one window were narrow; the lit hearth-fire, which was on the floor in the middle, was banked low. It was several moments before their eyes adjusted; when they did the first thing that held their gaze was a table, just to the right of the door, stacked high with clay pot containers, copper pans, and bundles of herbs. Herbs hung from the rafters too – as did an assortment of animal skins. And there were heaps of animal bones in the corner next to the bed. Skulls too. Hair, fur on some. Some small-human shaped – or children?

'Monkey skulls,' said the witch-girl, noticing Robbie's sucked breath.

Honey picked up a skull. 'Bat?'

It was the first time Honey had spoken since they entered the clearing.

'Clever,' said the witch-girl. 'From the moment I saw her I thought, here's one who knows.'

'Knows what?' said Alice.

But the witch-girl ignored her; was again fighting for breath – like a fish out of water, thought Robbie. 'Sit down,' she gasped. 'Please!'

They sat: Robbie and Honey grabbing the two stools; the witch-girl on a bench. Alice stomped across the floor to a flat-topped narrow chest; almost as soon as she had settled her bunched skirt, she sensed something in the chest move. She gave a little shriek.

'That's Puff,' said the witch-girl casually. 'Puff's very fine. A very fine – snake.'

Alice leapt up. The witch-girl walked past her, lifted the lid.

In moments the snake's head appeared. An adder. 'Poisonous,' said Robbie.

'I do know!' cried Alice, taking shelter behind him.

The snake hissed, heaved itself up further – then poured its body over the chest's side like water from a jug, to reach the floor.

It got no further. The witch-girl's walking stick deftly lifted it up. And the snake seemed to acquiesce. Its hiss became half-hearted; its tongue flickered only briefly, then retracted – the stick returned it to its home almost effortlessly.

Home or prison though, thought Robbie. Is some witches spell about to put us in a similar box?

Almost as if responding to his thoughts the witch-girl said, 'It's no prison. Once Puff's had his mice he's happy. You'll be happy too once I feed you.'

And, having closed the chest's lid, she went to the fire, ladled out pottage from a large black cooking pot, then brought out cakes – and then pork dripping to spread on them. While they ate, all too hungry to care what potions might be hidden in the food, the witch-girl settled herself by the fire, hunched her knees up to her shoulders, and after a bout of coughing and some settling of her breath, attempted to explain.

She wasn't a witch. She said that several times. Not, anyway, the sort they probably imagined. Wise woman, white witch: these were possible names – but not just witch. Not a daughter of the devil. Not that.

'My name's Winn,' she said. 'Until two years ago I lived comfortably, was the miller's daughter, in a village. Not far from here, half a morning's walk. Less. When I was thirteen, two years ago, a terrible sickness struck the village. People died. Many people. My family...' Her voice trailed off, her eyes, already overlarge in her pinched face, widened – as if they were about to burst with sadness.

Eyes very like Alice's, Robbie thought. Blue, but otherwise... He looked across to Alice; kept looking – wanting her to catch his look, send her a reassuring smile. She was focused on the food bowl, empty now, clasped still in her hands. But then her eyes lifted – she stared back, startled, quizzical. Then her face softened. Something in his chest fluttered strangely. He dragged his eyes away. He said to Winn. 'So you came here? After your parents died?' but his tongue felt big in his mouth, like a cow's.

'Old Peck's house. Yes,' said Winn, swallowing hard, avoiding his face, intently poking with her stick a guttering log at the edge of the fire. 'It was my aunt brought me. Death was calling, but she thought Old Peck could stop up my ears – be wise-woman enough to get me well. And she recovered a good part of me – but she couldn't recover my breath.'

'But where is the old witch? I mean Old Peck?' said Alice, nervously.

'I was with her when you arrived. For two years I have been her apprentice; now... Now I tend her grave.'

'She's dead!' cried Alice.

'She is with God. She was old. It's the way of things. This winter's last gasp was hers too.'

'Well my father wasn't old!' shouted Alice, her face furious. No one replied.

'And everyone's sitting talking, and no one's saying it... and...'

Alice flung the bowl at the floor. Then dropped to her knees – violent, convulsive sobs burst out of her.

Honey, sitting nearest, shuffled away; Robbie stood up, stiff, embarrassed. And looked imploringly at Winn.

Pushing away her own sadness, Winn lifted Alice up into her arms, hugged her, began a gentle song that grew and keened – into a sound like a squall thrumming ship halliards and sheets, Robbie thought. Nevertheless, Alice's shuddering eased. Her hand went to her mouth – she began to suck at the knuckle as a young child might. After a time, utterly exhausted, she slept.

'Soon it will rain,' said Winn – laying Alice down onto a heaped bed of straw. 'Tonight, you must stay here.'

'Your powers stretch to looking further into our future?' asked Robbie with a wry grin.

'Some things... This I see. That Alice, when she is just a little older, will wield a great power over you.'

'Really! Well sorry, but, honestly, I don't think you can see far into the future at all.'

Within the hour, Winn's predicted rain arrived. And quickly grew fierce. Darkness came early.

Alice slept.

It wasn't especially cold but Honey, Robbie and Winn settled close to the fire. Winn smeared a thick green ointment over Honey's nose to sooth its aching and confirmed it was broken. Honey talked about exacting revenge on those hunting her: ways to first hurt then kill. She favoured using trees. Her people would bend back sapling trees, she said, tie bad men to them, cut the twine holding the trees down, tear the bad men in half. Robbie winced, talked up love, mercy, the Christian way: forgiveness of enemies, turning the other cheek. Mercy was weakness, Honey said. Forgiveness too. Honey tried to say – her face now stern, scornful; words increasingly impassioned – that in her world necessity governed: the strong survived. Take, kill, eat – acknowledge the debt of your need as you kill, share to console the spirit world. But, when you must kill, you must.

To Robbie and Winn it was hard to follow, difficult to gather the sense of it. Honey still lacked understanding of many English words. The rain beat down heavily in the silences as she drew frustrated breath before stuttering on.

'English people follow strange God, not world isn't it,' she concluded, her voice rising close to a level of shout. 'That wrong. Not right way, isn't it!'

Winn closed her eyes. Her hands moved up to cover them; then moved down to her chest, clasping together as if in prayer. She was breathing slowly, now making soft whistling and humming noise – as if summoning and imposing serenity, Robbie thought. And was succeeding: for Honey had fallen silent, Alice had stirred and half turned over but hadn't wakened, and now he found he was listening to Winn's murmurs transfixed. When finally her eyes opened, the fire's shadows moved off her face, and her pallor left.

Her face, bathed in fire-glow: radiant – Robbie gasped.

Winn said, 'Granted, there are to be found many echoes of God in Nature. But, Honey dear, Nature alone isn't God.'

Honey gave back a long unblinking look.

'Now that... that sounds wise to me,' said Robbie hurriedly, fearing Honey might turn violent – that he wouldn't put it past her! 'Wise woman!'

'Wise girl, hopefully,' laughed Winn. 'A girl who believes we are the ones in Nature with God breathed into us.'

'No God in bad men,' said Honey sulkily. 'Bad men, my world, we kill. Cut skin from body with shells, make person swallow live snake, pull...'

Winn coughed. Then took hold of Honey's hands. Gave a gentle squeeze. Decided the moment had come to change the subject. 'So tell me, my dears, what has brought the three of you to my world? Time now for the whole of it.'

Robbie explained.

Winn listened appalled, her face returning to chalk white, her thin lips purpling– as if the blood had left them.

When Robbie finished, Winn stayed very still, unresponsive, as if in a trance. It was many minutes before she spoke.

'They won't give up looking. They will be looking now. You must leave here with the first light of dawn. I will give you food for your journey. I will point you the way. I'm only sorry I'm not fit enough to go with you.'

CHAPTER TWELVE

THE ATTACK

Honey was the first to hear the man. She awoke exultant, from a vivid dream. The female deer in it. The deer's throat slashed open by her own hand. Deer blood spurting onto Alice…

The door, giving a sharp creak as it opened, was in the dream – but it brought her awake. Something… someone was there – sidling over the threshold.

Too dark to see.

She kicked Robbie. He groaned. Rolled away from her.

But the dream's potency simmered: with a blood-curdling shriek she launched herself, wrapped her arms around legs, pulled tight.

The intruder crashed down. Headfirst into the fire's embers – screaming as a chunk of smouldering log burst, sprayed heat and ash into his face.

Alice, sitting up, screamed too.

Winn got hold of Alice's wrist. As more men entered the room, Winn dragged Alice into the blackest corner; Honey instinctively joined them – but scattered embers were causing the floor-straw to fire. And the next man in carried a burning rush-light in one hand; sword in the other.

The room flooded with light – but the first thing the rush-light man saw was his companion, hunched up, blinded, fighting pain. And for a moment he hesitated, and in that moment Robbie got hold of the burned man's dropped sword and thrust it at the other's belly. It cut deep, went in a long way. The man's mouth gaped – pain shrieked out of him. Robbie twisted the sword, yanked it back. Something like red twine came. Blood flowed.

Robbie stood frozen, stunned by what he'd done. But rush-light and sword fell – and then the man toppled.

As he dropped, others entered, took hold of Robbie before the shock cleared him, and advanced on Winn, and Alice, and Honey.

But the floor-straw between the girls and the men was burning more. And Winn flung Puff out of the chest at the nearest man.

And something else at the flames.

The flames soared.

~

Five.

Five men.

Robbie counted. Counted again. Five!

And hunting dogs.

Winn's rain had stopped.

He tried to weigh options. Seek a way out. Plan escape.

All of the men, it seemed, had made it back outside. One had been blinded; the one Robbie had stabbed was probably dying. Two were clamped onto Robbie's arms. The other, fighting smoke-sting, ran round the back of the house to see if the girls could have got out. Robbie thought that if they were there he must find them. There was plenty of light to see by. The house was ablaze; the thatch had caught.

The collapsing roof made the flames intense; the heat forced the men right back to the clearing's edge – brought the conclusion that three black-blistered, turned-to-charcoal bodies would be all they'd find when morning came.

CHAPTER THIRTEEN

IN THE WELL

'We jump,' said Winn: bent double, gasping to find breath, coughing.

'I can't.' Alice said. 'Can't!'

'We're out of the house… but this is… is the best hope… In the forest they'll track us… Have dogs…'

'Jump, isn't it,' Honey said.

They were at the well. Alice was sat on its raised top-stones. A hole, black as night, gaped.

Behind Puff's chest the hut wall had been built deliberately weak. Winn's tutor, Old Peck, had rarely been free from enemies: narrow-minded types who'd never tried to understand the base-knowledge of her craft. Most years there'd been those who should have known better than to call her a devil's lackey – but didn't.

Winn had thrown Puff, then sulfur, then kicked out her heels at the wall's thinness. A hole came, big enough, just, to squeeze through. Winn shovelled Alice. Honey went.

Then Winn – feet and a leg scorched by flames.

'In seconds they'll catch us. Alice, jump.'

'No!'

Winn pushed. Alice tumbled. She crashed twice into the well's sides before she hit water.

In the water, she went down: hurting terribly, terrified. She had never learnt to swim – and when the air in her clothes brought her back up, Winn, arriving, smashed onto her, knocked out what was left of her held breath…

It was Honey who got Alice back to the water's surface; it was Winn's hand that found Alice's mouth and stoppered her choking cries.

Honey clung on to Alice, holding her tight, supporting her; Alice sicked water out into Winn's hand: coughed, gasped, spluttered.

And suddenly understood that she had to be quiet.

She battled to calm herself. When the panic began to ease, astonishment replaced it: Winn wasn't in the water.

Honey's breath was rasping against Alice's ear. Winn was saying something in a loud whisper but Alice couldn't catch it.

And it was too dark to see anything.

Eventually, Winn's hand guided Alice's. There were iron rungs in the wall. Alice pulled herself upwards, found that Winn was on a ledge, about a foot above the water's top, a narrow area undercut into the rock, a space only big enough to kneel in.

Winn heaved Alice to her. Alice found that the narrow space went back, that it was deep enough – just – for the two of them and Honey.

'No noise. No sound, whatever,' coughed Winn. 'And we'll stay alive.'

Winn's house burned. They heard its crackle and collapse for what seemed time out of mind. Winn coughed and coughed. Winn thought the fire-noise was hiding it. 'Best I empty out now,' she muttered.

Alice murmured that the well must fill with smoke – and the fire's ferocious heat.

But it didn't.

There was the reek of damp soil and wet stone. There was the earth's marrow-bone cold. Numbing cold of saturated clothes, too.

'Clothes we take off,' urged Honey.

They had few to remove. They'd been sleeping in undergarments – there'd been no time to grab anything else. But Alice's fingers wouldn't work. She was shivering, shuddering: with wet and exhaustion and dread. Winn and Honey had to strip her; she didn't protest.

They pressed against each other for warmth. The embarrassment left quickly: comfort and heat came from the intimacy.

And the clothes proved helpful: Honey used them to blanket Winn's coughing – pressed them tightly down, over and around her face whenever wheezing began. Sometimes they went on Winn's now blistering feet and leg.

Waiting.

For the men to leave.

For dawn to come.

And quite often they thought the men had left already – before sun-up. Then the sudden growl of a voice, or a dog's whine, or a horse stamping ground, arrived hard as a slap.

Sometimes they slept.

Alice lifted her head from Honey's smooth as silk, clammy-warm shoulder. Dawn brought mist, drifts of grey and white, and she watched the trapped stuff near the well's top – mist looking like sheep's wool caught on briars. And though she remained cramped tight against Honey, she got her head a little further out into the shaft, watched the mist fluff about, and found herself wondering if it hurt when sheep's wool snagged – got itself torn off. Which was an odd thing to be troubled about, she thought: it was difficult to care much about sheep: they lacked character, were never inquisitive like pigs and horses and dogs were. As dear, dear Peg was.

She resolved to be kinder to Peg – when she got home.

When…

But then she wondered if she were going mad. That she wasn't thinking about Robbie and should.

Why wasn't she worrying about him? Her letter to him had caused his capture to happen. She thought, how horrid she'd been towards him too. And that he might already be dead….
She closed her eyes.

Mad…

Was she?

Odd shapes jagged about under her lids. She watched them, followed their patterns, thought how very like they were to the mist patterns above her.

Thought how she liked to make patterns.

And the turmoil eased a little. And she thought, if I am mad it's because of the way my mind works: it flits about, connects things that ought not to connect…

Not my fault…

And, anyway, she'd begun to be nicer to Robbie – hadn't she? She'd tidied herself up at the stream, made herself look good – for him.

Had he noticed? She thought not. And she lifted her eyes to look up again at the wool-mist swirls.

And from out of them, let down on its rope, came a bucket.

Winn sensed its coming, even as Alice gasped. Then Honey did. All pushed hard in against the ledge's back and against each other. Alice felt tension trembling through Honey's body.

The bucket splashed down, dipped.

Filled.

They heard water sloshing back out as it rocked, the going-up pull rushed, careless. They feared a second filling must come. Breath held burst.

They heard:

'Drinkable?'

'Looks it.'

'We'll have to bury Tom. We can't carry him and manage the boy.'

'We should kill the boy. He don't matter. It's the Princess that we want, ain't it.'

'If she's not dead we might need the boy.'

'Don't see why any of it matters to the Cardinal. What's it to 'im anyway?

'Ours not to reason…'

'You know more than that. You always know stuff. You find out.'

''Appen I do.'

'So!'

'It's the Cardinal and Queen Katherine ain't it. Plotting thick as thieves. Keeping Spain sweet. Hurting the French. And something to do with the papacy, I'll be bound. Something the King's not to know. As usual.'

'Keeping it from the King!'

'That's what I said. The Cardinal has ambitions all of his own.'

The Cardinal?

Wolsey. Has to be, thought Alice. And though her heart was thudding in her chest, and the terror induced by the men's voices clawed so hard that she could hardly breath, she forced herself to listen harder – biting her lip until she tasted blood. She was the one best qualified to understand. Of the three of them. Had to be! She must make sense of it. It was for her to do.

The men though had begun to move away; their sound – now something about her father: that the King never liked him, wouldn't miss him – was fading. Alice squirmed with indecision: should she climb up? Get closer?

Different voice – another man joining. Alice strained to hear. Heaved herself out onto the iron rungs, began to climb.

She heard: 'Water is it? Give. Christ's blood I'm hot. But there's nothing that looks like whole bodies. Not a bloody thing. There are charred bones. Two skulls that look human – no eyes. Some hair. But not much. Not much joined together skeleton either – and those 'eads.... don't seem big enough to be them. Even the bones…'

'And you'd know! They were girls remember. No big bones in girls.'

'Look for yourself.'

'I will. 'Cause if they're not there, we'll have to get moving bloody quick.'

'Which way?'

'The boy'll tell us.'

Robbie's voice, distant, strained: 'I won't.'

A pause. A cry of pain. Then Alice heard: 'Sonny, before we've finished with you you'll be begging to tell us everything you've ever known.'

CHAPTER FOURTEEN

TWO BREAKFASTS

Five horses. Six dogs. Four men and Robbie. Two horses, being led.

Heading east – briskly.

They slowed as they caught sight of a church's tower top. A village – finally – reached. They would make a stop there, they decided. Just for a little while. Refresh.

In the vast open space of the shared field closest to the travelling road: village folk. Tending, cosseting not-long-up beans and peas. Not long up. And their emergence, their vivid green shoots randomly punctuating the harrowed soil-brown, brought every year, awe; and heartfelt relief voiced in prayers to May's ice saints. And gratitude: warm as painted letters in religious books – their priest, last Sunday, said.

But seeing the travellers' approach, men and women, children too, paused, straightened backs, rubbed and scraped soil, sticky still from the overnight rain, off hands – shared concern.

Agitated.

One, two, then all, downing tools, leaving the children, hastening to the houses. From the road Robbie saw, and his heartbeat quickened. Someone might help him. Someone, surely…

His gaze latched onto a man running, the bailiff, he thought, or the bailiff's messenger, sprinting fast, faster still. To the manor house, presumably, to inform the lord.

For armed men, even if known, ought not to be trusted – everyone knew: it was a rule, vital as God's Commandments.

The villager's lord, noting Robbie's hands roped behind his back, legs tied, said, 'Good morning gentlemen. Your journey I trust goes well? Who is this young man, your prisoner?'

'An enemy of my master.'

'And who might that be?'

'Sir Harry Burfield. And he's doing the Cardinal's business. And the Cardinal's doing the Queen's.'

'Queen Katherine, you say. And yet … Cardinal Wolsey I care not for. A butcher's son. Ain't no breeding in him.'

Robbie's hopes rose. He drew breath to speak, interrupt, explain. But dread stifled sharpness; his dry throat choked: words stuck – stuttering, rasping oddly.

He managed little of sense before his captors grabbed him. They wrestled his head down onto the mane of his horse. Held his head there. Pulled a blanket tight over his face.

'The devil's words are in him, my lord. It's why the Cardinal wants him. To interrogate. The Tower will loosen his evil tongue, reveal his acolytes. Weird daughters of Satan.

Listen to him at your peril. He has clever words to rot your soul.'

'Then the Cardinal is welcome to him.'

'And to be pleased about your help, when we say. We'll not linger long. We stop only in anticipation of hospitality, of breakfast. And the horses rubbed down.'

He was taken off the horse. The blanket remained – and was tied, the rope worked into his mouth to muzzle speech. When men were brought food and drink, he wasn't. He tried to steel himself: told himself it would be no worse than a punishment beating at school – if they made use of their breakfast time to begin to extract information.

Torture him.

They hadn't yet.

But they kept arguing about it. And though the consensus thus far was that interrogating and torturing could wait, that they should return fast, report in, it was never unanimous. And from time to time they'd argued whether the girls really were dead. Though no one seemed able to explain how, in the name of all that was holy, that they couldn't be.

Robbie kept telling himself that they weren't.

He'd remembered Winn's animal bones. Those had to be the bones that the men had found. The animal bones.

At least, he supposed they were animal... He still wasn't sure what to make of Winn... He'd trusted her because Honey had.

But Alice didn't trust Honey.

He shook his head, back forth, this way, that, trying to shift the blanket, loosen it. It was wool, not very closely woven, kersey, not broadcloth, not scarlet: he knew quite a lot about cloth; his father shipped it out, sold it on; it was England's best export – and his father's...

The blanket over his head was kersey. Certain. There were gaps in it, pinpricks of light coming through. But he couldn't really see anything. Tears in his eyes too, now – that he shouldn't let be there. It wasn't manly. It wasn't...

It was the sudden thinking about home. He thought, I ought to know better, I must do better.

He shut his eyes. Squeezed the lids tight.

To get a grip.

It didn't help: his head spun, there was dizziness, sickness – like the sick feeling that began deep in his stomach's pit when he'd been in a boat on a rough sea.

Who to trust? rattled behind his closed eyes as if his skull were hollow.

And opening them, he thought: perhaps, the men, his captors, were working for some just cause – for surely if anyone in this world could be trusted, a cardinal could. So, perhaps he should trust the Cardinal. Trust that Wolsey would make everything right. Then he'd need only to explain.

And believe that Honey would, for now, take care of Alice.

Except – his every instinct urged escape.

Find Alice. Find Honey. Be with Alice.

How? The men kept his hands tied behind his back; and his legs they roped to the stirrup straps of his horse as soon as they started to travel. They hadn't even freed him to pee.

He ached, he stank. His linen undergarment gave little protection from the rough of the horses' saddle and flanks.

Cold. Scared.

But surely, he thought, there'd be a moment when the men's guard would slip. He'd yet to meet men of their sort who'd remain vigilant for long. He'd stay ready; the moment would come – when it did, he'd take it.

Winn said, 'I'd think he's the sort who'd risk escape. He'd try to escape.'

'Yes,' Alice muttered. 'I wouldn't. Couldn't.'

'I think you could. You climbed to the top of the well to listen to the men.'

'That's different.'

'Not really.'

But she thought it could be true. Winn seemed to say trueish things.

She'd felt calm within herself, felt Robbie-like pride too, since she'd edged to the well's top, listened, observed, reported back. Her crying self was done, she thought – and this resolve, since made, had trickled and dripped drops of quiet calm that ought really not to be there: given everything that had happened. But they were. And it was, she thought, like the sensation of being in the warm water of her monthly bath, squashed up but snug in the wooden tub – one of the servant girls squeezing water from the washing cloth so that it dribbled down onto her back and shoulders. And this she tried to explain to Winn – and was surprised and pleased that Winn listened earnestly, didn't poke fun. She felt sure Robbie would have.

She and Winn were sat protected by trees in patches of sunlight close to Old Peck's grave. The still smoking remains of Winn's house were out of sight unless they stretched to see. They were trying to rest, recover. Honey was close by, feeding a cooking fire, boiling freshly laid hen's eggs and, whenever she could, rhythmically plucking feathers from a dead chicken to a lullaby-like song. Winn, having wrapped around her burns rags made wet with some strange something, now pronounced herself satisfied that the pain was going, and moved closer to Alice, began to comb Alice's hair, using fingers to do it.

'You have lovely hair. Long and fine. As most girl's do. A girl's hair is a powerful tool with which to bewitch men. You must take good care of it.'

'Is that why married women have to keep their hair covered?'

'It is kept as a delight for their husband.'

'I don't ever want to get married.'

'Robbie expects you to marry him.'

'Robbie's just a silly boy.'

Winn laughed. 'And you're no longer a snivelling girl?'

'No, I'm not.'

'Good. So now you just need to lose your perpetual frown.'

'I don't have a perpetual frown. I don't! … Do I?'

Alice had twisted round, was peering curiously into Winn's face. Looked for a long time. Winn smiled. Raised an eyebrow expressively. Alice giggled.

Honey brought to them each a boiled egg. At first Alice kept hers in her hand, it felt comfortable there, and she absorbed its warmth and shape, rolling it back and forth.

When eventually she broke open the shell and dug her fingers into the yellow yoke, scooped it up into her mouth, she thought it the best breakfast egg she'd ever tasted. Ever! And Winn said, 'Alice dearheart, when your pained, worried look goes, your eyes entice and positively glow. Your eyes could be better even than your hair – be your very best bewitching tool. Men, Robbie, would be as wattle's daub in your hand.'

'And your kindness is yours. Though not a tool of course. A… a… thing. I don't know the word I want. But I know you make me feel safe – even though this can't be the safest place. The men-at-arms will come back. Or other ones. Soon. There must be lots out looking for us. Lots.'

Winn said calmly, 'No, being here right now is our best bet. If they suspect you're alive they'll think you'll have run far. They won't look here.'

'Do you truly think that? Perhaps you're saying it to keep me positive. Because we have no shoes, no kirtles, skirts, gowns. Running anywhere is hardly an option.'

'That's not it.'

'Or perhaps… perhaps…' Alice hesitated. Realised she was about to say something spiteful. Very pleased that she hadn't. For it was another indicator that she could push her old self aside, wasn't it. A smile flickered.

'What is it now?' asked Winn amused.

'No, I shouldn't say.'

'But you really want to.'

'No, that was the old me. Not the now.'

Winn laughed. 'The new-formed you. Just like that!'

'Now you're mocking.'

'Yes. Sorry. Quite right. I shouldn't. But tell me anyway.'

'No.'

'Go on.'

'Well… I was about to suggest that the real reason for staying here is… is because you haven't any breath to run.'

'I see.'

Alice saw Winn's face harden. Wished, wished she hadn't told her. Winn passed a hand across her forehead.

'Yes,' said Winn carefully, 'I can't get far very easily – true. I have to gather my strength before I try – and go slowly. But we're also here still because the first part of my plan has to begin here.'

'Your plan?'

Winn drew in a deep breath, kneeled forward, cupped Alice's face in her hands, stared hard. Alice blinked, then closed her eyes. Winn waited until she'd opened them. Very deliberately Winn said, 'It's good you are being braver. Before this is over you may need to be braver still. But we all come at bravery from different starts. It's easier for some than others. Often the most imaginative find it hardest. They see clearly all the possible perils. The future is a maze of uncertainty to such people. Relationships too. So the way for them to go forward is one step at a time. Not look too far ahead.'

'You're telling me to go one step at a time.'

'I am.'

Alice became cross. 'Well, I can be even more brave. For a start I'm being brave about these.' She pulled up her undergarment, ankles to waist, gestured at the livid scrapes and blackening bruises across her thighs and legs.'

'We've all got bruises.'

'Not like these.'

Winn looked more closely. Alice's right leg's skin was shredded raw, a two to three inch wide line from just above the knee to her hip – the well shaft had hit hard.

Amazing, Winn thought, that bones hadn't broken.

She endures pain well, Winn decided. It's fear of life's unknown, that scares her so.

'One step at a time,' Winn reiterated. 'And step one, is to fix this leg.'

Winn got to her feet. Smiled. 'Some of my soothing potions, ointments, the ones stored in clay pots seem to have survived the fire. I'll go and get something for you. And supplement it with something I'll fetch from the herb garden.'

Alice looked alarmed. 'You're not to leave me for too long.'

'Honey's just there. You're to make sure she doesn't eat all the chicken – and after we've all had some, I'll introduce you both to my pigeons.'

CHAPTER FIFTEEN

THE BARGAIN

As journeying recommenced, Robbie found it hard to stop looking at the villagers' hostile faces. The blanket had been taken off his head, but it seemed clear there was little point in trying to get them on his side; their minds were made up: they believed that words from his mouth might contaminate them. No, he wouldn't even try.

What he thought was, bide your time and stay strong. Because either he would get away, or the Cardinal would eventually help. Stay strong – a phrase he could flash up, easy to remember, access. But he found it hard to lift his gaze from the village people. And the thatched houses. The tower of their church.

Out of the window of one house: a pole with bits from a bush attached. It signified a Brewster, a woman who made ale for sale. There was, just for a moment, the thought that he might never sup ale in an alehouse again. Or be in a village again.

But then he told himself he would.

And, turning his head, looking back to the church, he decided he must focus on prayer. Starting with Saint Cuthbert. For of all the saints, Cuthbert was his particular favourite. It was the connection with the sea. Cuthbert, apparently, would stand knee-deep in freezing seawater for hours, chanting the psalms, watching the moon. Which was sort of mad, but also the sort of thing he himself sometimes did – though without the psalm chanting. Ship songs sometimes…

So gentle and kind was Cuthbert – a man devoted to helping the afflicted – that it was said sea-otters would come to him on the beach and dry and warm his feet with their fur.

Unlikely, Robbie thought, to happen to me anytime soon.

Because, he believed, he had good awareness of his own strengths and weaknesses, reckoned he had a long way to go before coming anywhere near to being the man that Cuthbert must have been – but most weeks he prayed to Cuthbert to give him the strength to bear hardship. And he liked to think that Cuthbert was pleased by such persistence; pleased that he was singled out. There were hundreds of saints.

But today's bargain would be with Cuthbert: get him out of this predicament and he'd devote his life to kindness and gentleness – with Alice.

Winn was introducing Alice and Honey to her pigeons. Her affection for them and pleasure in their existence puzzled Alice. Pride had suffused Winn's face; her eyes still remained bright with it – a hard gleam like the glint in the eye of the bird she was cradling. Alice was finding it hard to contain irritation. She'd never cared for the fluttering unpredictability of birds. She felt excluded.

'Birds are cold, and unfeeling,' said Alice.

'Eat good, isn't it,' shouted Honey.

Honey was half way up in a tree. The loft where the pigeons were kept was built into the tree. Kept away from the house. Safe from prying eyes – and foxes. But the fire had damaged the ladder Winn used to get up to it, because it was kept behind her house. Honey had climbed the tree's branches, helped Winn to climb up the ladder's scorched, blackened, weakened rungs.

Winn had brought a bird down. To show Alice.

Explain stuff. Explain that the birds were homing pigeons.

There were six; two were from another wise woman's home and caged. 'Each wise woman,' said Winn, 'has two such. Each pigeon has a ring into which a message can be put. One of the two kept caged is Patch. If we release Patch, she goes to the nearest wise woman west of here; Mottly, that's Mottly there on the pole sticking out – there Alice dear – he'll fly to the nearest wise woman east of here. Which allows us, me, other women of similar sensibility, to keep in touch, stay safe. We can send warnings, request help, arrange to meet and exchange knowledge. Not all the women can read, of course – after all, very few people can. But we have little shapes that we draw, that indicate things like danger or send the message on. We fly the pigeons on a regular basis, every couple of weeks or so, whether we have need or not – and then meet and exchange. Women such as us have learned always to be on our guard. And what it means is, I should be able to relay a message all the way to London. Perhaps even make contact with the King.'

Alice gave a mocking laugh. 'The King's not going to take notice of some wise woman, even supposing she could find a way to get to see him. He'd have her burnt as a witch.'

'Alice, dearheart, there's always a woman that a man, even a king, will take notice of. We just need to make contact with the right one.'

Alice snorted. 'And you won't be able to write very much.'

'That part is true. We will have to decide very carefully what we say.'

Alice frowned. 'You mean it don't you. The King!'

'Yes I do. If what you said you overheard is true, then King Henry's chief minister and Queen Katherine are doing something they shouldn't. Today, shortly, Mottly is going east, and Patch west. Patch will bring us some help, a meeting with a friend – hopefully some clothes. Mottly will start the London relay.'

'But I still don't see why the King would help us. Help Robbie! The King wouldn't!'

'Alice. Alice dear, calm down. Stop trying to plan far ahead. What is it you're supposed to do?'

'A step at a time?'

'Just so.'

Winn wrote: Wolsey plots with Spain. Wants kill Princess. Warn King. Then Winn drew the symbol that meant, send on – for those who couldn't read.

Mottly, released, went fast. After just a few climbing circles he was off, becoming a grey speck in moments, disappearing eastwards into a dazzling blue. Winn explained that Megan, the wise woman to whom Mottly belonged, might well come upon him before half an hour had passed. The message could be spotted, transferred to a new bird in moments. If everyone on the eastward relay route noticed their bird's arrival home reasonably quickly and acted with speed, the message, transferred to the next pigeon carrier, something like eleven times, could by nightfall reach a London destination.

'If it's not taken out of the sky by some rich lord out hawking, or a hungry eagle or some great owl,' said Alice. 'Or it rains and wet destroys the ink, the parchment – both. Or one of the birds changes its mind, goes somewhere else. Or one of the women's taken for a witch, arrested, tortured, hanged.'

'You left out, ends up as pigeon pie,' said Winn.

'One step at a time, isn't it,' said Honey.

⌣

They hadn't stopped at any more villages. They'd passed through one and glimpsed the church tower of another, distant, not on their road, off up along a winding track.

Villages were, Robbie thought – trying to calculate how far he might be now from Alice – generally found some ten or so miles apart. In which case, probably, they'd travelled twenty miles, perhaps thirty – since leaving Winn's. Thirty miles on a cart-rutted, dust puddled road, which the overnight rain no longer softened. A gloomy, closed in road too most of the time, trees right up to the edge of it; trees, trees and more, casting shadows. And from the length of those shadows now, it must be, Robbie thought, late afternoon.

There had been stops. Food. Water. The horses rested. Then walked, led – sometimes. He found it hard to walk, the land moved much as it did when first stood on after a long voyage at sea. He wasn't used to horses. For although the riding of a horse was no longer the sole preserve of the nobility, as it had been in olden times, when their role was the defence of the weak and maintenance of justice, he had rarely ridden – and wasn't especially keen to. So he wouldn't, he told himself, have wanted to be an olden days' knight – even though, unlike his family now, they paid almost no taxes. Because their function – the nobility – was to pay with their bodies and property in time of war. For which reason, a horse then was a powerful symbol that lifted nobles visibly higher than other men.

Of course, once married to Alice he would be expected to have such trappings; and their children would have every chance of being accepted into society's top strata. Though he wouldn't.

But did that matter? In the end it came down to behaviour – doing right as God wanted it done. So if now he escaped, sought out Alice, shielded her from harm – that was knightly.

But if he were a knight, he thought – settling on it, happy to continue to lose himself in the train of it – he'd make his visible symbol a ship.

He knew, a knight should have two horses: a destrier bred for war, rode only in battle, led to battle by the knight's squire; and a palfrey, more conventional, but better than a nag, which the knight rode when not in battle. So perhaps he would have two ships, a ship built for war, and one for trade; the war one the protector of the other. King Henry himself was building ships meant only for fighting.

Because, why not? The world was changing – and the pace of change had quickened in the last forty years. Men and women other than the nobility, from the middle, like his father or Cardinal Wolsey, had found ways to grow in wealth, knowledge, importance, power. Those of the middle sort, particularly the few elected by their peers to attend the King's occasional Parliaments, could now wield considerable power.

Ships not horses – any day of the week! Especially as just now, he hated horses with a passion.

And ships he could think about all day long.

And then they turned off the road. Were there. With his prayers to Cuthbert yet to be answered. His captors said: Sir Harry Burfield's manor house.

~⌣

It was more like a castle than a manor house. It was fortified. An unusually wide moat encircled it. There was a drawbridge. Portcullis. It would, Robbie reasoned, be a hard place to break into; it would be a hard place to escape from.

He looked and looked, trying to force in the detail. He told himself, stay strong.

Over the drawbridge, through the gatehouse, spyholes and murder holes and a stair way going up – and then a small square courtyard: gabled buildings on all sides against the crenellated stone. There were very few people about; those that were, looked away fearfully. He tried to catch their attention nevertheless; he wanted as many people as possible to know he was there. As the horses stopped, he filled his lungs, shouted, 'I'm Robert son of Rowland Walker, the Bristol merchant. My father's rich. He'll reward any who...'

It was as far as he got. The nearest of his captors, the leader, struck Robbie with his sword hilt, whacked it across the back of Robbie's skull. He had taken care to keep Robbie alive, but his patience was exhausted – the man Robbie killed had been a good friend.

Robbie slumped forward onto the horse's head and blacked out. Because his feet were still tied to the stirrups he did not fall.

It was dark when he woke. Raging thirst and dreadful pain in his head and chest woke too.

He cried out. A door creaked. A chink of light.

He saw he was in a bare, tiny room, just straw on the floor and a bucket. There was a small window close to the floor, with an iron bar down its middle.

The light waved, entered. A fat hulk of a man came with it, carried it. Robbie cowered, then made an effort, tried to sit up. Man and rushlight swung dizzily, side to side, like a church bell in a tower, clanging.

'Sweet Jesus!'

'Not yet,' laughed the man, squatting on his haunches, peering at Robbie with powerful intensity. 'John, your host, your warder.'

'My warder?'

'Warder. For to keep you whole and hearty is my job. To keep your tongue from paralysis is my job. You'll soon be meeting some people wanting answers to their questions. So best take a swig of this.'

The warder proffered a leather bottle. It held wine. Robbie managed one large gulp before convulsing, coughing.

The warder snatched the bottle back not wanting it spilt. Drank some himself.

'These people,' spluttered Robbie. 'If I don't give the answers they want, I suppose they'll torture me until I do.'

The warder looked hurt. 'Bless you, young sir. There's no general law in England that allows torture.'

'Good, so…'

'No general torture. In the Tower. Tower of London, however.'

'The Tower!'

'Best to be informed, lest you fetch up there. Traitors in the Tower can be tortured for information. And heretics to save their souls.'

'But not here?'

'Bless you, not usually. Though it is easy enough. If I were to take cord and bind it tight around your thumbs until the blood spurted from beneath your nails, why then you would experience excruciating pain – yet it is as simple to do as breathing. Or I could hang you on a hook and hang weights from your body. Or I could double you over and squash until the blood flows out of your ears and nose.'

'I suppose you're trying to frighten me?'

'Don't need much to try – judging from the look in your eyes. If you take my advice you'll answer every question.'

'Do you have other advice?'

'I was told you killed a man. So most likely you must hang. My brother is the hangman in these parts. He ties the knot and exacts the most slow strangulation. Death has been known to take an hour. So go to it with a jump so that you swing. If the body swings, death comes faster.'

'I'll try to remember that.'

'Kindness is my middle name.'

But gullible isn't mine, thought Robbie when John left.

But the light went with him. And after an hour or so of pain and fret, his last shreds of hope too. Saint Cuthbert hadn't responded – yet. Except, deep down he knew that Christianity really wasn't about striking bargains – the: you do this and I'll do that stuff. He knew his mum would be first up in the queue to remind him.

He tried to picture his mum saying it. But her face seemed to belong to some other time so long past. He lay on his back, stiff with fear, falling in and out of sleep.

CHAPTER SIXTEEN

---◦---

BURFIELD

'I'd say my softening up stuff's beginning to do the business. Usually does. Startin' to trust me like his dear mum.'

The warder, John, was reporting to Sir Harry.

'But I don't need you to waste time on him. Neglect your other duties. Why didn't you report sooner?'

The warder's face, cheerful moments before, clouded. Confusion played. 'My lord, I thought I was to find out all I could. You said nothing about damaging him. You said...'

The warder's head sank down; tremors of fear suddenly in him – his face reddening. Because, Sir Harry was a man encompassing contradiction: one of those men who'd be nice as pie one minute, choked full of fury the next. It was dangerous to fail him. Or just to misunderstand him. Bloody dangerous...

So the chaplain's interruption that came now was unexpected and brave. 'My lord, we've been here an age and only written "Your Grace",' said the chaplain.

Sir Harry reluctantly turned away from his twitching

warder. The chaplain was just yards from them, at the writing desk – a truly fine desk: oak, tall, the writing-onto-bit set at an angle: for ink flowed best if the quill were held almost horizontal. Clever wooden clips too, to hold the paper or parchment; and there was a weighted string to keep lines straight; and several trays and recesses that held an array of quills. And a penknife – because at the completion of almost every line the goose feather nib would need to be trimmed.

Sir Harry couldn't write well, but he was exceedingly proud of his desk – and he liked to stand close and admire its use. Chat with the chaplain. The chaplain tried always to respond with enthusiasm and acuity, knowing that Sir Harry liked to portray himself as a man of the new learning, someone who could slip into conversation that he'd heard about More's Utopia, or Plato's Republic. Sir Harry took care to be seen with educated people – Cardinal Wolsey types; Sir Thomas More types. But as the chaplain knew full well, Sir Harry was also, unlike Sir Thomas, a man of little conscience: unscrupulous, underhand – therefore a man to whom the Cardinal had increasingly turned whenever work on the edges of legality needed to be done. The chaplain tried if he could, to soften Sir Harry's blows – deflect anger. It was a contribution of sorts; helped him sleep with an easier mind.

'Is it just to be "Your Grace"?'

'Shut it,' snapped Sir Harry. And spun back towards the warder. Took a great menacing stride. Saw him cringe. Enjoyed it... And yet...

The letter did need finishing. Had to finish it tonight. Wolsey needed to have Sir Harry's news. It might do Sir Harry great good.

Sir Harry flung out an arm, let his open hand pass close to the warder's face. 'You, out! Go. Back to your stink and your nastiness. Before I change my mind.'

'Yes my lord.'

The warder retreated. Sir Harry turned back to his chaplain. Became milder. The letter took shape.

Your Grace, although the princess remains at large her recapture should not long be delayed. My intelligence gathering suggests that she is either headed for Bristol or more likely - now that I have the meddling boy - back to Sir Lionel's estate. The boy turns out to be the son of Rowland Walker, something which I am sure will come as no great surprise to Your Grace. You may prefer to use your own people to watch Walker, but if not I can provide. The man Matthew remains in my pay at Sir Lionel's.

As for the meddling boy, unless Your Grace wishes it otherwise, I will leave him in his cell to rot. Without food or drink death will come, but it will not be quick. And if his shouts of despair are heard, then rumour will spread that there exist certain matters in which such as we are not to be crossed - which will be to our mutual benefit.

Yours most bounden.

Burfield.

CHAPTER SEVENTEEN

ROBBIE ALONE

His strident shouts bring no one. He has hauled himself to the door, banged and banged with his fist. Eventually he collapses, cries: sobs, violent as his anger, crushing the breath in him; shooting pain over bruised ribs. So that he ends up curled, legs drawn tight against his chest, head tucked close to his knees, sucking a fist in his mouth – murmuring stuff: often about Alice: much of it confused – about love.

Sometimes he sleeps.

And quite often, he wakes when it is still dark – but he doesn't mind that: he prefers it when darkness engulfs him, obliterates him. But tonight he crawls on elbows and knees to the window.

It is an opening no bigger than his head, set inches from the floor, an iron bar through its middle. Tonight, moonlight is out there beyond it, giving form, forwards and down, to a bank of mud and the moat's surface; up – with nose pushed against the bar – the night sky, patches of low cloud in it.

The moonlight shapes a narrow road across the moat: like

a way out – mocking him. The wind's smell carries the promise of rain.

Rain arrives with the dawn. He has slept by the window and he hears and feels the rain without bothering to open his eyes: the rain plashing into the moat; the wind drifting a fine spray over his face. Probably, he decides, he will not bother ever again to open his eyes; there is nothing in his cell worthy of the effort of looking; better if he does not open his eyes.

He moves his hands instead, clasps them together on his chest, a gesture to stimulate repose; it is where hands go before the winding of a body into a shroud. His hands feel ice-cold.

He tries to will his whole body numb, his mind numb – extinguish the movement of his lungs. The light strengthens a little, but he does not open his eyes. Sleep, oblivion... He stiffens. A moist, cold something is touching his face. Wet and cold – and breath.

His immediate thought is of a demon. The devil, Beelzebub, is known to send such beings into the world to torture the weak, to tempt the weak; demons are often reported taking the shape of animals or birds. He keeps his eyes tight shut.

The wetness (a nose?) and the breath remain. And a noise follows, a rolling, continuous, contented noise like the suck of surf on a shore – a purr. Robbie opens one eye, then the other. Two bright half spheres stare back, very bright black beads set in liquid yellow-green, quizzical: cat's eyes.

The cat's eyes are an inch from his own; they remain even

when he tentatively moves a hand to touch the cat between the ears. A further stroke causes the purring to deepen, the cat to dribble, then butt its chin against his.

The cat inches forward. It is half in the window, half out, then over Robbie's face – Robbie does not move. The cat moves on, settles heavily on Robbie's chest, licking Robbie's hand with a small pink tongue sharp as a thistle. Evidently it is used to people.

Or is it just that he remains so still? Even wild animals can be friends, Honey had said.

Honey had made friends with beavers, apparently.

He keeps still; he does not want the cat to go away.

Perhaps, he thinks, Winn has sent the cat. To help him. Everyone knows that witches have a particular way with cats – and Winn is a sort of witch. The cat has come to bring hope. Winn wants him to know there is hope.

The rain falls faster; light barely penetrates, the air is damp, grubby, cold – but he feels braver because Winn has sent the cat. He shivers, the shivering jars pain into life, so many parts of his body ache. The cat remains though, on his chest, content, generating warmth that revives and consoles.

Content, the cat stretches its two front paws languidly, stretches them right forward to be either side of Robbie's neck. A claw scratches and catches in Robbie's hair. He closes a hand gently over the paw, and they remain still, paw in hand, the cat gingerly stretching out its claws, but unafraid, happy, purring still, dribbling still.

More rain falls. The cat, Robbie decides, most probably – if Winn isn't still guiding it – has stayed to escape the rain. He continues to stroke it, massage it; the cat rubs and stretches and purrs until it can endure no further pleasure. With suddenness that surprises, it jumps off, moves to a corner of the cell and begins to lick and clean itself with vigorous, methodical gusto.

Sitting up, watching the cat – now it is manicuring its claw-nails, biting, cutting, shaping each with its teeth – Robbie becomes repelled by his own filthy clothes and flesh. He beats his fists angrily on the floor, then rolls over right to the window, pushing his arms out as far as they will go, letting the rain saturate his skin, scourging his nails up and down to scrap the dirt free. He watches the rainwater, tainted by his own filth, running down his arms. It disgusts him. He withdraws his arms, wraps them around himself. After a time he drifts into sleep.

That the cat has gone is the first thing he notices on waking. The rain has eased; that is the second. Then footsteps – down the flight of stairs that lead to his cell. Boots scraping briefly on the floor outside his door. There is a cough. The door slowly opens.

The warder has come only to gloat. No need for interrogation, he says. No need for torture. They've sent men to Bristol; they know who you are, because you shouted it out. Probably won't even need to hang you.

'Some food and drink then,' says Robbie. 'For pity's sake.'

'Been told not to feed you. Been told to let you starve.'

When the warder leaves, the ringing echoes of his boots recede agonizingly.

Prayers resume. Most to Cuthbert.

CHAPTER EIGHTEEN

JACTA EST ALIA

Alice pulled the kirtle down over her head, tried not to take a breath until it was settled on her shoulders, tried not to smell odour that wasn't her own.

They had waited a day, and then another. Winn's acquaintance, friend, cunning woman, wise woman, white witch, black witch – Alice couldn't decide on a best word fit – had brought three kirtles and three gowns. But they were peasant quality cloth and far too big.

She hadn't brought shoes.

No shoes. A day and another – and those were, Alice thought, hours and hours wasted. But she said nothing. She must, she told herself, not make fuss, act disturbed. She would do as she was bidden.

'Horses and men go this way, isn't it,' said Honey.

'You can't know that for certain,' said Alice. 'I think my home is the other way. We should go there. We can't help Robbie. Just us. We are just three girls. Whatever can three girls do!'

Winn laid a hand on her arm.

'Picture a monastery fishpond,' said Winn.

'Why a monastery's?'

'Well-tended, well stocked – usually big. Picture a calm day, the water surface smooth, undisturbed. And the fishing monk waits and waits and sees no fish. Now think of a fish, pike perhaps, or perch, surfacing to take a mayfly. The water's disturbance is so slight the fishing monk on the bank sees it not. But the ripples spread outwards, wider, wider and wider and reach the pool's edge. The fishing monk takes note and knows of what he does not see.'

'We, how you say, eat flies?' said Honey.

'No,' said Winn, ' but we must have the faith to disturb what we cannot see and let our ripples spread.'

'But the fly is dead,' said Alice.

Winn coughed – fierce, wheezy, painful convulsing coughs.

On his knees, by the tiny window, Robbie prayed. He bent his head and closed his eyes and an image of the cat came unbidden.

The cat had not returned, but something of the hope that it had brought lingered. And so he prayed – and after a time there came to him imaginings: Saint Cuthbert stirring and twitching as the prayers arrived. And then, he imagined too the prayers, like solid things, as if illuminated on vellum, swirling out through the cell's window, borne aloft as if on the wind, travelling through whatever to wherever.

Cuthbert's earthly remains were entombed in Durham Cathedral. He knew that Durham was many leagues north.

He wondered if his prayers had to pass first into the tomb.

He liked that idea. It would be like a harbour, a gathering place of ships and safety, like Bristol's harbour. He imagined Durham's cathedral to be like Bristol's.

He had been with his parents. It was the town's largest building, greatest space. It's beauty, he remembered, remarkable; its hushed emptiness: extraordinary. Because, Mum said, it was never really empty, but filled with hundreds upon hundreds of years of people's conversation with God. God's too – with people.

Going there always gave him shivers like those of fever – a fever's giddiness also, sometimes.

Possibly, probably, he thought, he was giddy with fever right now.

Later, praying still, he sensed arrival at Cuthbert's tomb, saw the oil lamps that burned above it flicker, the bright cloths and wine bowls and dust and jewels that surrounded it glow. He felt awareness of something surging there.

And opening his eyes, he believed that something had changed. That something was different. But he didn't know what.

～

The pigeon's owner lived on London Bridge, at the Southwark end. The house was twenty yards from the pikes onto which traitors' heads were placed. The pigeon lingered there, on an eyeless, almost fleshless skull, for several moments – pleased with itself for finding its way home; recovering breath. Then it was off, beating its wings hard, noisily, to rise quickly to the food waiting in its home-space – the place accessed through a fist-sized gap in the plaster just under the roof eaves of the house.

The house was one of the bridge's tallest, five storeys, home of a wealthy merchant. The merchant's widowed sister lived in its top floor; and he strove hard to keep her there – well fed, with many comforts, but removed from socializing with his friends and family. For since her husband's death, she'd dabbled in potions, consulted and fraternized with astrologers, sought horoscopes and crystal gazing – calling to her certain spirits and angels.

She, not approving of his disapproval, kept her distance from him – and his wife. The pigeon's tidings, however, suggested that her brother might, for a change, need to acknowledge her existence and usefulness – take notice. Moneymaking was the wellspring of his life. She wasn't at all sure, but she thought the message, found tucked into her pigeon's ring, might well be hinting about disruption to trade. And even if it wasn't, she could play her part by laying the stress of it there. She believed the part was hers to play. It fitted her interpretation of several recent dreams.

Tonight, she would seek out her brother at supper.

'Jacta est alia,' she murmured. 'The dice are thrown.'

Three men. Wolsey's men:

'We should break in.'

'Persuade the mother to tell. I've a tried and tested line in persuading women.'

'Ee 'as that. I've seen 'im.'

'That so!'

They were bored to distraction with waiting. Fidgety, irritable to the point of exploding, now looking daggers at each other, fighting to control their tempers. They were not used to inaction. They had been holed up in the house directly opposite Robbie's parent's house for most of a night and a day. They had already taken out their frustration on the house's usual occupiers, a man, woman, their daughter and two servants. All bar the servants had now been killed, the woman especially slowly.

Rog, the most agitated of the three, spat down a great gob, said, 'They're bound to know somemat ain't they.'

John, nominally in charge, stared into Rog's screwed up, hating face with eyes that didn't flinch. 'No. For the umpteenth bloody time, no! Our orders were to do nothing to them unless the girl arrives.'

'An' what if she 'as. What if we just 'av'n't seen 'er. Gregory was asleep on watch. Last night. Asleep. I caught 'im.'

Gregory gave a simpering smile. 'I was just resting my eyes.'

'I can make that permanent.'

'You and oose army!'

Rog, fingered the hilt of his knife. He wasn't the sort to back down. He'd been fifteen when he'd killed his first man: at the battle of Flodden, 1513 – and hadn't stopped killing since. At Flodden he'd killed at distance, with his longbow arrows, but he'd been close enough to see the Scottish king James hacked down. The English, though outnumbered, had won a great victory on that day – and Rog had discovered he wasn't scared to snuff out life. Most people thought about heaven and hell. Rog simply reasoned that he killed on someone else's orders. His paymasters would be the ones visiting the devil's flames.

John stepped between them. 'Boys! Roger. Gregory. Grow up. Killing each other wasn't part of the Cardinal's orders.'

A crooked grin split Rog's face. 'I'm not scared of you John Wag. But I respect orders. The Cardinal's orders.'

'The butcher's son,' giggled Gregory, nervously.

'Our boss,' said John reproachfully. 'Thomas Wolsey, Lord Chancellor of England.'

'Yeah. Right.'

Robbie licked the moist, damp walls. He told himself, whenever it rains I can cup rainwater in my hands. This is England. Rains most days.

He pondered how long he could endure without food.

In the latter part of the afternoon the cat came back.

He placed a hand on its soft neck. The cat deepened its purr. To kill the cat seemed like a betrayal of trust, but, he reasoned, God had put creatures on the earth to serve man, to put food in his belly, to set an example of order – the work of ants to shame the lazy, the order of bees to advise disposition in man's kingdom; the hierarchy of angels…

And yet, he thought, the cat's a friend now – and possibly sent by Winn. And I've never, ever heard of anyone eating a cat…

With sudden, rigid decision he released his hold.

The cat arched its back, stretched languidly, left.

The London merchant: sat with his wife and two children. Through the door, his sister edged quietly in, following a servant. For several moments she stood in shadows watching them eat. Their candlelit faces were animated; their hands were kept busy tearing at meat, bread. Conversation was flowing, only interrupted by swallowing, chewing – and snorts of laughter from her brother. Ever the self-satisfied, priggish man, she thought. Forever talking: talking words without listening. Somehow, tonight she would have to make him listen.

She stepped forward, managed a smile. 'Brother dear-in-my-heart, greetings. And wipe away that scowl. There is at work a conspiracy to strengthen the power of Spain; a conspiracy against our King. Affairs that are certain to have a knock on effect – that will hurt trade; and thus may hurt you.'

'And just how the devil would you know?'

'Because we are all of us just five or six persons removed from someone who does. You, I am sure, are just six persons or so from the right someone. Someone who can warn the King.'

'Of nothing but the speculation of your addled brain?'

'Just make some discreet enquiries. Think of the rewards if I'm right.'

'Think of the fall if you're wrong. If we wrongly accuse. For the diseased tooth of a sufferer cannot be extracted without pain and the diseased soul of a criminal cannot be expunged without torturous pain. Slander the King's ministers and we shall be set in the pillory with an ear nailed to it, cheek burned with a red-hot iron. And as for your witchcraft...'

'Hush brother. You are frightening your children. It is not witchcraft that uncovers this. Worry not. And anyway, I am not a witch. At least, not the sort of your imaginings. Rest assured of it. Let profit be your guide.'

CHAPTER NINETEEN

TELL THE KING

Robbie rolled onto his stomach – into a thin wedge of sunlight, face pushing into the window space until his head stuck between the metal bar and wall. He worked his eyes; the green of the grass on the bank, and the blueness of the moat seemed strikingly bright; his eyes ached looking, but he kept raking, searching. And listening, trying to pinpoint sounds – people. From time to time there would come faint snatches of conversation – but he had yet to see anyone.

For a while, any voice, any spoken anything, triggered reaction. He shouted, I am here. Robbie Walker. Here!

But the shouting exhausted him.

He slept.

When he woke it was darker. Grey clouds and black; the wind up. On it, he decided, was the smell of approaching rain. Which, if it arrived, he must drink and drink – each and every blessed drop that his hands could take.

He pushed himself up onto his knees, closed his eyes to counter the dizziness that came, mumbled prayers of gratitude.

And reminded himself, stay strong. Think about Alice and Honey. Winn too. But, especially, Alice.

Picture her… But, all that came was the white delicacy of her face, and the worrying, vulnerable look: the one there so often in her large, dark eyes.

Alice… Troubled Alice… But no matter, he told himself. Once they were married he'd do all that he could to make her safe, erase the frowns, the terrors. Above all else, it would be a duty to God. Marriage was one of the sacraments, one of the Seven – one that was particularly appreciated by God – his mum said. Usually when reminding his dad…

There was a tomb she'd – his mum – taken pains to point out to him. It was in a priory church. They'd been on a journey, accompanying his father, some business, stopped for the night at the priory, enjoyed its hospitality. And she'd shown him the tomb, two people in it, important people, knights, lords, that sort, husband and wife, an image of them both depicted in stone, lying side by side, his hand clasped in hers. His mum had made him trace with fingers along the stone of each forearm down to each hand – told to do it gently, to gain appreciation of the gesture's tenderness. Because it – that gesture – was a reminder of the sacred bond made at their marriage ceremony, when each clasped the others hand in God's presence, to signify consent: and their acknowledgement that marriage is holy. Remember it Robbie, his mum had said. Promise.

It was the month before his first visit to Alice's house.

He began to hear the rain's patter. Then a sudden flurry.

He opened his eyes, made to thrust his hands out into the

wet – but before he could, the black cat sprung through, as if catapulted from a cloud. Holding something in its mouth. Something…

It dropped the something. Pawed it.

Meat? A bird? Something birdish… cooked from the look of it – snatched, presumably, off some kitchen spit or table. Bird – cooked undoubtedly, definitely: chicken… partridge?

He made a kissing noise with his lips. 'Good cat.'

Heart pounding, straining to move carefully, he inched closer. Feet. Bottom. Shuffling. Until near enough. Just needing to fling out an arm, risk the grab…

The cat stretched, arched its back, as if expressing satisfaction, as if saying, see how clever I am. I've brought you a present.

'They'll be closing the gates, any minute. Evening's just about here. Towns, castles, manor houses pretending to be castles, manor houses, always close their gates just before it gets dark.'

'Mine doesn't.'

'Exception to the rule. If we go in now, we might not be able to get out. We should wait until tomorrow.'

Alice and Winn were standing outside Sir Harry Burfield's manor house, on the side furthest from the gatehouse. A moat separated them from its high sentinel walls.

Alice said, 'This moat's ridiculously wide. Widest I've ever seen. But Honey could swim across. There'll be a way in somewhere that's not the main way. Honey swims like a fish.'

'Of course, Honey swims,' said Winn doubtfully.

'Better than…' Alice shuddered. Huffed breath onto cold hands, beat her arms against her sides. '…anyone.'

They'd left tree cover when the rain that had fallen for the last hour slackened, but the poor weave of their cloaks hadn't kept it from wetting through to their inner garments. They were soaked through, teeth chattering as they spoke. Winn was leaning hard on her stick, face ashen, exhausted, lips trembling.

Alice observed her, full of dread. Alice was trying to be brave – stay positive. Be determined as Honey. Honey had straight away jogged off, to work round the edge of the manor house's moat, seeking out other ways in and out. She had little understanding of the strengths and weaknesses of fortified stone places. But Alice's father had rescued her from the Tower, so anything was possible – she'd said.

It had taken four gruelling days to get to Burfield's. Honey had tracked, and the few villagers and other travellers encountered had, when cajoled by Winn, said stuff that had led them there – but Winn hadn't been able to move fast: because of breathlessness and coughing fits. And not having shoes: her feet – though soothed by salves, bound up with rags – remained horribly blistered by the fire.

And, of course, they'd had to keep watchful, hide at the approach of people on horses, make shelters and sleep away from the road. It had been hard to stay brave and positive about that.

Honey was an expert at making shelters though: bending the branches of bushes to make a frame, filling in with leaf litter, bracken – she didn't even seem to mind the creeping, crawling bugs. But Alice did. Bugs –and the forest's darkness; and the dreadful things that must lurk there. She'd needed Winn to hold her very tight in order to find sleep; she'd had to be wrapped in Winn's cloak, covered head to toe, and hugged. Which helped – but often Winn's raking coughs disturbed and alarmed.

Last night, worryingly often.

'Tomorrow' said Winn. 'No argument. Tomorrow we make certain he is still here, work out exactly where he is, make a plan.'

'I think,' said Alice, now staring fixedly at the grey, uninviting waters of the moat, 'we should wait for your pigeons to do their stuff.'

'No guaranties that they will. The pigeons were always a long shot. Any rescue's almost certainly down to you and me – and Honey.'

'That's ridiculous.'

'Not at all. In the morning I will forage in the woods and put together bunches of medicinal plants. Then we, you and I, not Honey, will approach kitchen staff, servants. We will offer the plants in exchange for information. Kitchen folk always know everything about everyone.'

'But then what? Once we know… where Robbie is?'

'To be decided.'

'But you'd have to find some way for rescue, and there can't be anything. There wouldn't be any way to do something like that on our own. I really don't know why we've come all this way. I don't!'

Winn said, in a low, disappointed voice, 'One step at a time.'

'No.'

'Alice?'

'No!'

Alice stamped forcefully, foot to foot – and anger burst out of Winn. 'Ungrateful, ungrateful wretch. I feed you, shelter you. My house is burned to cinders because of you.' Her voice rose. 'I have no family... my tutor, mentor has died. I have staggered here, miles and miles and miles and...'

She was shaking her head violently, breathing heavily. Her walking stick dropped out of her hand. She sank down onto her knees and began to cry.

Alice stood open mouthed, shocked. From day one, Winn had been a proverbial rock, soothing presence – someone she'd instinctively trusted to know what to do. But now... Alice felt sick inside. Let down.

Uncertainty seethed in her.

Suddenly she thought, I must step up, grow up. It's a moment to. Show strength. Hug Winn. Say sorry. Say, I was wrong, I'm so sorry Winn

She clenched her hands into fists, dug her nails into her palms, strove – but at once her voice cracked and the sentence began withered. She couldn't manage it. Because: which words....? This one, that? She couldn't decide. She thought only that everyone hated her. They all did. Her eyes filled with tears.

She turned away, and a gust of rain blew hard into her face, her hair streamed out and fell back, slapped wet and cold against her neck. She shuddered. And couldn't, couldn't decide what next to say.

She took to her heels, fled – back towards the road. And back up it – she decided. Back and back and back.

'Your Grace, she wishes to speak with you.'

'Not now.'

The king, Henry, spoke quietly, with authority, but the twinkle of mischievousness that was sometimes there in his eyes was absent. And that was a concern. Probably, this was the wrong moment, Norris thought. And yet… The King had just unhorsed his opponent. He ought to be in an excellent frame of mind. Usually, such times were the very best of times.

Norris retreated a step. But only one. He waited, standing tall, backing himself. The King, sat still on his jousting horse, began to drink thirstily from a flagon handed up by an attendant.

Norris's king, Henry, was a king in his prime: twenty-nine years old, successful, popular. He'd ascended the throne determined to be remembered kindly by posterity: he'd worked hard to excel in the knightly pursuits of jousting and courtly love. And he'd succeeded in war.

But that was seven years ago.

Seven years ago, looking to please, particularly, Catherine his Spanish wife, but also his Spanish in-laws and his own subjects, he had waged war against France and Scotland and won handsome victories. Now, egged on, encouraged by his chief minister Cardinal Thomas Wolsey, he was playing a different game, playing the peace card – he was now seeking to unite Christendom in Christian-like peace. Consequently, he was awaiting a visit from the Emperor Charles, before travelling to France for an unprecedented meeting with the

French king, Francis. England and France were, of course, the bitterest enemies, fighting each other for hundreds of years. But if he could bring peace, and then fight a crusade, his chivalric fame would be assured.

Not surprisingly, a meeting between the King of England and the King of France was not something of which Emperor Charles approved. Charles was presently en-route from Spain to the Netherlands – the Netherlands being just one of his many European possessions – and he had determined to stop off in England, talk Henry out of his meeting, warn him off. By now Charles should have arrived, but a truculent north-easterly had kept him bottled up in Corunna.

If Charles didn't reach England by the 26th May, Henry had said, just this morning while selecting his jousting horse, to Norris, then too bad! For after the 26th May he, Henry, was travelling to France, no matter what. And once there, even if nothing else proved possible, he intended to raise, suggest, affect some policy that might loosen Spain's grip on the New World – loosen Spain's grip on America.

'Why you run?'

'I'm going home. To Mummy. You can't stop me.'

Honey had caught up with Alice. It hadn't taken long. Alice hadn't been able to run far – she was shuddering, fighting for breath, staring, staring at the mud and blood covering her shoeless feet.

'You come back. Rain going now. Rain going away. That way, isn't it.'

'Going east.'

'East? Yes, east. Where bad men come.'

'Not all of them.'

' Yes. London, isn't it. Bad men.' Honey lifted Alice's chin, peered curiously into her face. 'The men who kill your father.'

'I don't care… and it's: killed. Killed my father.'

Honey stood, frowning, fidgeting. She was not used to bargaining, reasoning. In her own country she'd simply have ordered that someone behaving as stupidly as Alice be beaten. Perhaps she should do it herself? Here, now. The thought pleased her. She smiled.

'There's nothing to smile about.'

Honey shrugged. 'Rain gone.'

'You say it as if you'd made it happen.'

'My people only make rain come – with dance.'

'Dance?'

'Yes. Dance isn't it. Now you come. Winn needs it.'

Alice said stiffly, 'Winn needing me is not the way things should be. She needs to be helping me.'

'Come!'

Honey clapped her hands imperiously, started back. She didn't look round, but she knew Alice trudged behind her.

'Your Grace!' Norris, persistent, pushing his luck – patting now Henry's horse, making an extravagant fuss of it. Because, Norris's heart was in his mouth – patting the horse gained him countenance. He'd told the Blount woman, Elizabeth Blount, told her that the king was especially bad tempered today. Bad tempered, even though he was jousting – which he loved. For the King was waiting for the Emperor's arrival at Dover. He hated waiting; hanging about.

Needed to be doing.

She understood all that, she said. Norris, sweetie, just get him to look at me. When his eyes meet mine he'll come.

There could be, she was sure, bewitching, manipulative power in her eyes. In her smile also – in all aspects of her lovely, so-expressive face. She believed she must still have it. Power over him. Henry, King of England. Even though their intense relationship had cooled since the birth of their son. But he, the King, was still fond of her, cared hugely about her.

She flashed him her most coquettish smile.

Mounted still on his horse he came over. Elizabeth patted its nose. Henry reached down, placed his hands either side of her waist and, with an easy movement that displayed agility and strength, lifted her off her feet and into the saddle. The pommel there made for a tight fit. She was squashed in, awkward, hurting – but she managed a thrilled laugh nevertheless, continued with bouncy smiles.

'Let's ride,' said the King.

They rode to the river – the Thames, not far. The king was staying and jousting at Baynard's Castle and the barge was tethered close to St. Paul's; crew and musicians close enough to call.

The sun was setting. The river sparkled with it. Elizabeth's eyes sparkled, one hand trailed in the water.

They talked of many things before the pigeon's message came up. The barge went upstream with the tide, was among the reed-beds and wet meadows of Chelsea in the almost dark, when Henry said, 'I remember that American princess.

Pretty thing. Funny nose. Don't know what happened to her. Wolsey was dealing with it. I don't know what Wolsey's been up to but it shouldn't take long to find out. Tomorrow. Tomorrow. There's something much more pressing for me, you, to do just now. '

'Better get on with it then. Thought I just felt a spot or two of rain.'

CHAPTER TWENTY

THE PECKISM

Thomas Wolsey, Lord Chancellor of England was at his London residence, York Place. With him, fidgeting, clearly nervous: a messenger sent by the King. The message summoned Wolsey to Baynard's Castle. Before the day was out.

'Why does the King want to see me?' Wolsey spoke slowly, softly, but there was unmistakable menace in his voice.

And menace in his movement too: he stepped away from his desk, made big strides towards Henry's messenger. Wolsey was a large man, a man who dominated a room easily. Now as he thrust his face forward, a face just now – because the rain had stopped, and the room faced south, and the emerging sun came strong – as scarlet as his cardinal's robes. Menace glistened like sweat.

Henry's man gulped. 'Your Grace, he didn't say.'

'You always know things, Richard. You always do.'

Wolsey brought his face very close. Richard winced. 'Your Grace, whatever I know it is not my place to tell.'

'Richard, Richard. There are things I know about you that

it's not my place to tell. But say them I shall – if that's what it takes.'

Richard backed away, darted a look, fought his unease.

'A cardinal's integrity should not be so fickle.'

'Richard. I'm no ordinary cardinal – as well you know. What would you have me do? Run the country on my prayers!'

'Perhaps.'

'Don't be silly. Just tell me what I want to know.'

~

Henry's messenger had gone. Wolsey paced the room. He'd not yet been found out, but the king was on his way to finding out. So decision time: damage limitation or go for it: pretend he was doing his best to find the girl, the American princess? Rescue her? Or kill her – and eliminate all those who were involved?

The light was going out of the sky when he decided: the second course. Kill. He had promised Katherine, the Queen, that he'd crush the plans of the English merchants trying to get a foothold in the Americas. The Americas belonged to Spain. The pope had decreed it.

Thus the Queen would be happy. Spain would be happy. Pope and cardinals too. God's main players.

God too… hopefully.

But first, messengers would have to gallop through the evening and journey on after dark. They could not stop. Rest. Not for a moment.

And if clouds hid the moon they were unlikely to arrive in

time to accomplish all that needed to be done: find the princess, kill all – and not leave any trace.

There was a sometimes-moon. Honey was to swim as soon as there was a good stretch of cloud, darkness enough to hide her – but there was (Winn's expression) a sometimes-moon.

They had to wait for it not to be there. When the moon's light touched the moat, the water's surface shimmered silver.

Honey had agreed, also, to wait for Winn's signal – a, the way is clear, signal. An owl's hoot. Honey thought it a poor imitation of an owl. They had argued about it.

Other arguments had raged, on and off, all day. Winn had been unable to push aside Alice's view that they ought not to be there at all; and it had nagged and slowed and worried like an aching tooth. Winn had been uncertain, hesitant. Honey, upset by Winn's negativity, had kept saying so, kept telling her to brave-up. Fiercely. With unflinching glares.

Winn protested that at least, today, she was back to trying. Unlike yesterday. Yesterday – she'd admit – she'd lost her nerve. Because: for four days she'd held fast to the idea that to go to the hunters' lair was best; that it would be the last place the hunters would expect them to be. But then they'd arrived – and the solid, gaunt walls of Burfield's fortress home had crushed her optimism.

And then, the confusion, disappointment, sense of being let down, on the faces of Alice and Honey. It had made her ashamed – and the shame refused to go, drained her, made her wretched, Though she told herself, she'd every excuse: she'd been utterly exhausted, soaked to the skin, in considerable pain.

And yet ... she couldn't lose the feeling that she'd bitten off more than she could chew. That she had succumbed to what the Greek philosophers of long ago called hubris – that the old gods were after her.

It was Old Peck who'd told her about that.

Awake for most of the night, she had sifted and searched through her mind for other pearls of Old Peck's wisdom. Appropriate Peckisms. Little had come. Accept for one something: her, when all else fails, keep buggering on. By which Peck meant, you must keep striving regardless, until your stars align. For good luck can only work when you put yourself in a place to receive it.

She'd greeted the dawn with that idea fixed. She'd gathered her medicinal herbs before the dew had lifted, slipped into the manor's courtyard while many there were not long awake, sleep-dregs hopefully slowing sharpness, and worked her way to the kitchens. Alice trailed along, but refused to speak to her or anyone. Winn did. She was fifteen years old, not too young to be taken as silly, not too old to be treated with suspicion. She wasn't beautiful, but she knew also that she wasn't ugly. If she cast off her walking stick, straightened her back, took care to regulate her breathing... Old Peck had told her often enough that there was an easy warmth in her eyes, a friendliness that couldn't but make her attractive. Ease of conversation too. She liked to chatter. Today her chattering had included much probing – subtly done, she thought – to tease out information about Robbie.

But the things told to her, increasingly convinced that there was nothing that she, or Alice, or Honey could do. Not at Burfield's.

Honey didn't agree.

Robbie, apparently, was in a room overlooking the moat. For Honey: chance enough.

Winn, crouching low, searched the battlements and windows near to where they thought Robbie was. She kept needing to cough. Her breathing was unsettled, surging, making her gasp.

But, between the half-stilled coughing she watched. From some of the windows, there was candle or rushlight flicker. Because of it, some light puddled the moat. Winn watched windows and window reflection for disturbance – and the skyline where it met the battlements. She had to be certain no one was looking out.

Alice watched too.

Honey waited. Far enough ahead to be out of their sight. She lay on her front, almost naked, hidden by reeds, ready to begin the moment Winn signalled. The moat's edge and ink black water was just a foot from her. Winn and Alice thought her plan madness. But then, they thought just to be swimming a kind of madness. Neither of them could – plus, they said: all manner of human waste went into that moat; it'd be too dark to see it, avoid it. Still worse though: lights' absence, could allow things, slippy, oozing eel-like alive things, to rise up out of the slime of its depths.

Anything could be living down there. You just didn't know.

They were both wrong, Honey said. Wrong.

And they needn't worry. She'd this swimming trick: she could clear her mind, make the her in her hide, think herself out of herself – she could become as a beaver.

Beaver. One had inspired her to swim.

She'd been about five, playing at a lakeside, suddenly entranced by a pebble found. She could picture the pebble now: skin-smooth, round as soft-fruit stones, its patterning swirls of brilliant colours. So caught up in it had she been, she hadn't noticed her sisters had moved on. That everyone had moved on. She'd been left alone. And suddenly, frighteningly been aware of something pushing through the near bushes: a big something, loosing a low growl: wolf, bear – big.

She backed right up to the lake's edge, water at her toes, then over her toes… And it was then that she'd seen the beaver, swimming almost effortlessly, its paddle tail speeding it towards its lodge. And she'd imagined she was one, a beaver, and begun to swim – though never, never in all her life before had she swum.

A sudden, raucous mating howl from a fox masked Winn's owl. Honey wasn't sure she'd heard it. And it hadn't sounded wrong enough to be Winn's. She waited several moments to see if it would come again. It didn't. She decided to go anyway. She was tired of waiting. But first she closed her eyes, worked her mind to form there a beaver's face, ears pushed to the back of its head, the small bead eyes, see-through eyelids, prominent front teeth, whiskers. Then the oiled waterproof fur, the webbed rear feet. Tail.

When she opened her eyes they were beaver eyes. And beaver like, she wriggled forward; the plant press against breasts and belly she barely noticed; the sap smell and mud stink she accepted.

She slipped down into the water, face first.

The water's cold wrapped – but there was beaver's fur now to slick it, ease shudders. She swam slowly, taking care not to splash, make noise – the strokes of her arms and legs stayed beneath the water's surface; legs locked together, undulated tail-like. As was a beaver's, most of her head was submerged. But, as she began to come close to the window gaps where Robbie might be, she had to restore her human voice, chance sound, call out Robbie's name, hope he would hear – and reply.

The moment she switched back to human, her teeth began to chatter. She called, but the whispered sound stuttered away, without penetrative power.

'Robbie…'

The thin noise reverberated, but seemed to refuse to travel, as if the darkness shoved it back.

She listened. Listened…

Nothing.

Where she was, the manor-house walls, tall and crenellated like the castle walls they mimicked, went straight down into the moat. There was no ledge of ground to haul herself onto. She had to tread water. As she listened, the sound of her own voice echoed in her head.

She'd made the first two calls beneath a window lit by some inner light. It was where they'd been told he was. Now she thought: if imprisoned he might not have light…. Almost certainly.

She decided to call beneath black window spaces. Not that there were many openings that could be called windows; most were arrow loops scarcely big enough to see into.

'Robbie…'

Nothing.

She began to suspect that the information they'd been given was false.

She swam a little further, called under other dark windows – carelessly now, frustration spilling out. Suddenly, she realised she was close to the drawbridge. It was down – someone was standing on it. To get under and past she took a deep breath, dived beneath the water. When she surfaced, the first thing that she saw were eyes of a cat.

The cat emerged from a window not much bigger than it, a window quite close to the water's edge. And here there was the thinnest sliver of land. Which now the cat was padding carefully along... Until it vanished!

There wasn't a splash. No cat in the water. But Honey couldn't see it. Here all was in the blackest shadow.

She was still close to the drawbridge, gatehouse, people. She dare not call out. She got her face right up to the window the cat had come out from.

It was a very small window; there was a bar of metal down its middle.

'Robbie...'

CHAPTER TWENTY-ONE

HONEY DECIDES

Robbie awoke with a start.

He'd fallen asleep while stroking the cat; stroking the cat had smoothed fears – brought the sleep. Now the cat was gone. And a voice was whispering his name – urgently.

Heart thudding, he crawled to the opening. His head spun with the movement. He believed the dream he'd been in couldn't have finished. 'I'm Robbie,' he said.

Delighted laughter came back at him. Briefly. Then suppressed. 'Me, isn't it,' said Honey.

'Sweet Jesus!'

Her hand, arm, undulated in between the bars. And suddenly there was the touch of flesh against his, and he grasped it, held on. Trembling.

She squealed. 'You no gentle!'

'Sorry.' He realized he was squeezing hard. Reluctantly he let go. He didn't want to let go.

Honey's hand withdrew. He put his head to the bar space. Couldn't really see her. Could feel her warm mouth-breath on his face.

'I go. Come back,' she said.

'Don't go.'

'Must go,' she said firmly. 'Honey will save.'

~

Except that she didn't know how. But then, just as she eased herself back into the moat, she remembered the cat. And pondered where had it gone... if there was some other way in, for a cat?

Of course, she was longer and fatter than it. Not too much fatter...

She pulled herself back out of the water, edged along the strip of ground in the direction the cat had taken. It was hardly wider than her feet, less in places; she had to spread her arms, hands, to grasp the building's stone, scrabbling for any depression, crack, crevice. The cloud had thickened. Moonlight and starlight was hidden.

Nevertheless, she thought, the cat hadn't seemed to have gone very far before it had disappeared; though the light reflecting back from its eyes was all she had seen – so possibly, probably, it needed only to turn its head inwards to have vanished. It might not have gone into the building at all.

When she reached the spot where she thought it might have slipped in, she searched all around, then stretched her arms as high as they would go.

Found nothing.

She edged along a little further.

A smell, excrement, piss suddenly.

And the wall jutted outwards. Here the lip of land ended.

Her hands explored. Reached round where the wall swelled. Reached down.

At the water's surface was a narrow opening. It was, she realized, the end of a shaft – a shaft down which, judging from the smell, human shit and pee came into the moat.

She tried to imagine the cat getting in. It would have to have got in from the water – wouldn't it? She didn't know much about cats. But she did know, animals that didn't usually swim were reluctant to.

She bent lower. The smell made her retch. Was it possible to get in and climb? She just wasn't sure if she could bear to try.

She straightened up, rested a moment – she leaned against the shaft, sucked in cleaner air. She felt extraordinarily weary. She closed her eyes.

Opening them, a new thought struck. The outside of the shaft tapered inwards as it went up. Just a little. Narrowed as it went up. Perhaps the cat had gone up the outside, not the inside? She couldn't really believe that a cat would want to go up the inside.

Spreading her arms and legs star-like, she hugged the shaft and tried to climb. If she fell, she'd bump down into the moat. There were grooves where the stones met, joined – the mortared bits. Her finger's skin became cut, flayed, ripped by the roughness. Legs too.

She inched up.

As the shaft's width narrowed, the climb got marginally easier. But her strength was failing; and her hands and parts of her legs were rubbed raw. Just when she thought she could go no further she heard sounds, people talking. And came to the top of it. And a window.

No closed shutters, no glass. Very narrow – but a cat could have got through easily enough. She must try and get her head in.

Her ears wouldn't go. Then they did. But the window ledge was wide, and even with her neck stretched as far as possible, her chin rested back from the edge. It was difficult to look down.

And too dark to see much anyway – though she sensed the closeness of the room's walls; and reckoned the floor must be about six feet below. Her every instinct suggested this was a small, enclosed space; a barren space.

Which, she decided, made it somewhere unlikely for people to be often in. So if she could just get down…

She thought that possibly, if she twisted sideways she might get her body through – but should she? She might get stuck, fixed in the window, trapped until discovered. Then she'd be pulled in or shoved out of it, ripped and battered to fall forward and be captured, or back to crash off stone and into the moat.

It was a point of no return. She must decide. Push on? Or go back?

She felt sick with dread. Ending up caught like an animal in a trap, would be the most terrible thing.

She remembered that once, long ago, she'd come across a kit beaver caught in a fishing trap – unable to get its mouth open wide enough to bite through the wood of it, shift the stone weights off it. Nose just above water, but utterly bewildered, not comprehending, strength draining, whimpering, whimpering.

Still a child herself, she'd struggled to free it. She'd shouted for help. One of her brothers, older than she, had come, laughed at her distress. And her many tears. Which had gone on long after they'd released the kit.

'I'd rather live with them than you,' she said. 'Do it then,' he said. 'I dare you.'

So she had: visited the beaver's home. Not that day but another. Soon after. Though it was something her mother and father and sisters and brothers – even the Shaman – all said she'd only imagined she'd done. That she could not possibly have, not really.

But she'd been swimming with the beavers regularly by then, visiting the lake most weeks. They'd got used to her; seemed happy to see her, would come up close, swim alongside. She was after all not much bigger.

Sometimes though, she'd get cross if they went away before she was ready to stop playing: far too often they'd resume prolonged underwater foraging, or, worse, return home – diving from her sight, vanishing into a place to which she had no access.

Her brother's dare fed into that crossness. One day, she swum over to their lodge, took hold of its twiggy dome, pondered, reflected, heard beaver sounds from inside it – and, with remembrance of her brother's dare ringing in her ears, suddenly, crossly, took a huge breath, and plunged down to the lake's bottom, making herself open her eyes – though she hated doing that then. But the water was murky, making it hard to see – she couldn't find the tunnel entrance; she flailed around, tugging at branches, lungs bursting...

Agony.

Beavers could stay under water ten times longer. No

amount of thinking herself as a beaver ever seemed to help with that.

So it was with breath almost gone, she'd found the tunnel – and had just moments in which to decide: go on or give up? For if she went on and got stuck even briefly, snagged by the tunnel's branches, she'd drown; but if she gave up, she would never try again.

And that was the moment she'd reminded herself that failure was for lesser mortals – that she was the daughter of Chief Steady Hand. His favourite.

Wriggling this way and that to ease the tunnel's tightness, she groped her way in, fought free of any sticks catching against her. And suddenly shot up into the area where the beaver's slept – their space above the water level.

Both the adult beavers were there – and several kits. Their horror subsided quite quickly; hers too. Eventually all had been well...

She made up her mind.

~

They began in daylight, but the third change of horses happened at dusk and there was still a very long way to go. It was a journey that would, on horseback, even with changes of horses every twenty miles or so, usually take two days, sometimes four – in the depths of winter a week. But as their boss, Cardinal Thomas Wolsey, had pointed out, they had to reach their goal by mid-morning of the next day at the latest. They must ride without pause; the message they carried would bring death, but death might well pursue them if they failed. The three men had nodded apprehensively, knowing full well that the Cardinal was a man who did not make such threats lightly; that if any man could operate outside the requirements of the law and smooth objectors away, he could. And would.

Three men. Because there was safety in numbers wasn't there? And they could stay together until they reached Sir Harry Burfield's manor house. Where one would stop. While another pressed on to the house of Alice's mother. And the other... 'Bristol my friend,' said the Cardinal.

Night when it first came was owl-dark: a hunting moon. Each messenger put into his hand a silver penny that Wolsey had given them. It had been dipped in holy water; it was a charm against elves and other evil.

The messengers hadn't ever seen the little people, or spirits, close up – but they'd sensed them often enough. They knew such things were out there.

She was going on. But her arms would have to go first. And if she moved her arms her legs had to hold her, grip the shaft. If she lost focus when her arms began to move and the grip of her legs slipped she would plunge back and her head would be torn back through the window's edge.

She murmured trance-like, stay focused.

She got her elbows to her chest, wriggled her hands up to her face, scraped them over her head, shaping them like a swimmer beginning the fast stroke. As her elbows rose, the pain in her shoulders made her gasp then squawk. Then her arms came free. She thrust them outwards to the walls and twisted her body sideways, pivoting on one side, the sill grinding against her ribs, and pushed her legs up off the latrine shaft so that her body shifted forward and worked her shoulders through. Her hands pushed hard, her body moved further.

Then her hips stuck.

She heaved with her arms, kicked air with her legs, scrabbled, wriggled. Her scant underclothing rucked and tore away.

She fell.

In.

Three feet, four, arms flung out trying to break the landing. She finished up on a wooden plank, seat covering, of a latrine – the shaft she had climbed up's latrine.

She rolled down onto the floor, sat slowly, stiffly up. She winced, blinked back tears, registered bruises and the flesh scrapped off hips, belly – discovered much of the skin of her fingers was rubbed raw.

Then listened. Above the thudding of her heart: women's voices.

Two women. Honey, on elbows and knees, eased open the latrine room's door, snaked out, edged along an unlit, narrow passage, found the voices getting louder – and began to smell cooking smells, hear kitchen noises. Then she reached what had to be the kitchen's entrance; wide, huge oak doors, wedged back.

She would need to get past. Beyond.

She stayed on her knees, moved slowly, made no sound other than breath.

The kitchen was lit well: there was a blazing fire, several rushlights. She could see two large tables, and a row of charcoal-burning stoves behind them. The large, open fireplace had cooking spits across it on their jacks; the two women were facing it, ladling things out of large cooking pots– steam and food smells rose from sops and broth.

Their backs were to her. She could get by…

But the patience of one of them suddenly withered in the cooking fire's heat. She cried, "Ot as the Devil's place today. Flamin' June's come early,' and began to pace. Mutter. Then add testily, 'Seems a great shame not to be able to take 'im any.'

'Oo's that then?' said the other woman.

'You knows right enough. You know. That poor boy in the cell below us.'

'E's not really a boy though is 'e. Almost a man.'

'Whatever!'

'Old enough to take the consequences of 'is actions.'

'What's 'e done then?'

'Dunno. Must be somat bad.'

'But just left to starve and rot.'

'E' doesn't 'ave to starve though. We send food down.'

'Warder eats it. Caught 'im. Twice. They want 'im to starve, but for no one to know. 'Appened before.'

'The least they could do is take 'im out and 'ang 'im… Shush!'

The woman's voice dropped away to a whisper. Honey froze. She'd continued edging across the opening, the pacing woman hadn't once looked in the direction of the door, she'd nearly made it – but the floor was slippery with condensation. A foot had slipped, her battered hands had grabbed at the corridor wall – pain squeezed out a squeal.

'What?' muttered the woman at the pots, turning slowly. 'Is it that cat again? Stealing food? I'll 'ave its guts for garters… Sweet Jesus!'

Honey realized she'd been seen.

She sprang up, ran. Just two strides took her out of their sight. But then, as she tried to sprint on along the fast darkening passage, half looking behind her, she crashed into an unseen wall. No windows, no light. Knocked down, stunned, she could only grope, on hands and knees, feel her way forward round the corridor's bend. And found another door off it, small, shut. She tried to pull back its bolt. Couldn't. Her hands hurt too much to grip. Time squandered.

Footsteps… Close…

She glanced back. The darkness seemed to pulse. She could hear a panting breath…

Honey snarled defiantly, bear-like – and staggered away. Both women were fat, slow. They wouldn't catch her. But now one was shrieking for help.

The passage bent. The woman's shrieks lessened. The passage ended. Stone stairs. Spiral – going up and down.

Up or down? Up might take her to the battlements; from there she could escape with a dive into the moat. Down…

She hadn't understood much of what was being said in the kitchen – except that some boy below wasn't getting food… She'd understood that.

Well, she'd come this far.

She started to go down.

CHAPTER TWENTY-TWO

PEACE IN OUR TIME

Henry, King of England, crumpled up the message just placed in his hand and threw it back at the man – Wolsey's man – who'd delivered it. The man let it hit him and fought hard not to react. He knew well, that was best.

Henry looked at him shrewdly. 'Your message says your master is too ill to travel. How ill would you say he was when the message was handed to you?'

'He has been often unwell of late…'

'And!'

'And so it would, on mere looks, be hard to judge – Your Grace.'

'But you'd suppose it to be his humours? Which? Too much black bile? Yellow? Too much phlegm? Moist Jupiter squashed out by dry, hot Mars?'

'I am no physician.'

'But one has visited? Your master purged? Bled? Or shall I send mine?'

The man stared miserably at the floor.

'Well! Speak up! Which?'

The man lifted his eyes, white faced. Struggling. But sudden movement at the back of the small room, ripple of attendants bobbing obeisance, stretched the moment: gave more time in which to think. And if it was the Queen, Katherine, he thought – as it probably must – coming through the door that led off to the dining hall, he had still a chance to allay suspicion.

For the King had come from feasting and entertainment. Wolsey's man had gambled that he wouldn't, that he'd accept delivery of the message in his dinning seat, calmed by the fug of eating's pleasures – and thus, get away without interrogation. It hadn't worked. The gamble failed. The King, when told of his arrival, had left the meal crossly. Fuming, even before reading the carefully crafted words of excuse, explanation, apology – carried to Baynard's Castle with Wolsey's instructions rattling between his ears as if his skull were hollow. Give nothing away Stephen; understand that time needs to be gained; make delay Stephen – some act of chivalry perhaps at some en route street (the King would like that) – or invent believable reason for pretended delay. And, Stephen, that … that I've entrusted you with this. You. Your cleverness, relied on.

He'd assured the Cardinal he could handle it; he was appalled that his tongue, just now, had frozen.

But the Queen might come to his rescue. She'd know she should – if she guessed correctly what this was about.

The Queen, Katherine, advanced, eager, concerned. She drew level with her husband, acknowledged with a careless flash of eyes the messenger's bow, then fixed on Henry an expression of earnest puzzlement.

'Whatever has Mister Ripon done to cause such upset? I heard your voice from next door. Shouting between courses leads to indigestion. And a particularly fine custard is next up. You would not want to not enjoy it.'

'Ripon here, has delivered a message. Wolsey sends word he is too ill to travel. He has dared not to come, though I sent for him to come. Hours and hours ago. With all speed, all urgency. I think he's afraid.... I think... think...'

Henry paused. She was aware of a change in his face, the acute consternation clearing – which was a look familiar; and there too often when first they were married. But she was older than he. She'd known then how to sooth a furrowed brow. Had abundant delights to do it with then.

She no longer thought she could. But she must try.

'Think what, Your Grace?'

'That, as you are here... perhaps that will do,' he said studiedly. 'To make a start.'

An imperious waft of hands emptied the room of all save the Queen. A glare brought the door shut and the feasting noise decreased. But now he waited, watched her. For any hint of unease. Guilt. She moved away from him a little, moved closer to the candles that, placed on a small table, provided the room's light. From the room's only window, a song drifted in. Someone in the courtyard below, a man, caressed a ballad. It was sung well, he thought; and Katherine's body began to sway a little to it, her feet making modest dance steps. She liked to dance. So did he.

'Dear, dear Kate, what have you and Wolsey been up to now?'

'Up to? I? Behind your back?' She answered, as she usually

did, with gravity. She rarely became emotional or flippant.

She hated a lie.

He searched her eyes. Blue and beautiful – the only beautiful part, he thought, remaining of her youthful prettiness: prettiness, swallowed up by her many pregnancies; and the sorrow of losing seven children.

She met his look, stared back, gently defiant.

'Henry, a Christian king should not succumb to rumour. Or petulance. How many times have I told you? It hurts you, just as much as you hurt others by it.'

She bent and took the message from the floor.

'Nonsense.'

'A king's duty is…'

He cut her short. 'None of your moralizing Katherine. Not now. Not tonight.'

She went to him, touched his arm. But the intensity of the anger, suddenly returned to his face, was such that it surprised her. Wolsey's message dropped from her grasp. As she made to pick it up, he kicked it away.

'Henry!'

'What have you promised him, Katherine? What? Is it that you'll get Charles to help make him pope? Is it that?'

'I… No, I…' Her voice faded. She crossed to the window – hoping to find some distraction, something to say about while she gathered her wits. But the moon had fled; the man who'd sung she couldn't see. Or anyone – though light leaked out of the building's many windows. Lovers meet in shadows, she thought, bitterly.

'Speak up!'

'Wolsey's helping Spain and me,' she muttered. 'It isn't

something I want. But… but better that, than that you and the King of France dance.'

'It is no mere dance. Our meeting, in friendship, King of England with the King of France, is unprecedented. It will long be remembered. Right now, six thousand men are at work preparing tents and pavilions and tilting yards and wine fountains, and satins and cloth of gold enough to dazzle the world. All the nobility of England will be there. You will be there. But it's to achieve something far, far beyond entertainment, Katherine. Christendom's peace in our time – through balance of power.'

'Is it?'

'Yes. And I shall seek other things, too. One particularly – which I believe Wolsey doesn't. So listen now. Spain – your nephew Charles – has its New World Empire. But the Pope bans exploration of and amity to, as yet, undiscovered lands by England – or France. I intend to change that. I, and the King of France. We. Because it's illogical. It's ridiculous. It's unfair. It's…' Henry let loose a deep, spluttering sigh.

Katherine had stayed by the window. She took a deep breath, let it out quietly. She thought, how can I not admire grand designs that seek out peace? She could all too well understand his frustration, his hurt. She turned.

'I'm sorry,' she said.

'Are you?'

'Yes. Because… well, it's that last thing that you said about. England joining with newly discovered lands. You are right. Wolsey is now working to thwart it. He has asked me to make sure Spain knows his part in that, inform my nephew, help where I can.'

'Thank you.'

She sensed the tenseness seep out of him. He took her hand. Led her to the door. Stopped.

'One other thing, Kate. It was on your orders that that American princess was locked up. Why ever did you agree?'

'She made me lose our child.'

'And who told you that?'

'Wolsey.'

'He's misleading you. Has misled you.'

'Where is she now – the girl?'

'I don't know. But I'm going to find out.'

Honey paused. The spiral stairs had ended at a narrow passageway, windowless, very dark – just a hint of light from somewhere up ahead. Shivers of fear ran down her spine. Everything felt closed in; she felt suffocated – unused to large, enveloping buildings. It was as when a bad dream engulfed her. She was desperate to be back under the sky.

But she had to go on. Above, footsteps were starting to clump on the stone stairs. Going up? Or down?

She thought up – but wasn't sure. Suddenly panicked, she ran full tilt towards the light. Flapped into a wider space. And there: a solitary candle-lantern; on a small table. And a man on a stool by it. Asleep.

At least, he seemed to be. She forced herself stilled. Looked hard for any sign of pretence.

His thickly bearded head lolled on his chest. His mouth was open. There were grunts, snores... Satisfied, she looked beyond him.

Behind were three doors – shut. Each had an iron lock. She

crept closer; close enough to smell the sleeping man's sweat.

Only once before had she seen a key go in a lock: when they'd put her in the cell at the Tower. And been so intrigued, she'd momentarily forgotten her predicament – and her anger at the insult to her person; the way they were treating her; the lack of respect.

But she'd teach them to respect her now, she thought. She'd get Robbie out, and then…

She inched nearer. Held her breath.

The man had a knife. Sheathed in his belt – but the hilt was towards her; she need only lean forward, heave it out.

Should she?

And use it?

She tried to imagine using it. She'd stabbed animals, hadn't she! A straight up pull and she could plunge it straight back down into his neck, shoulder even, if he woke.

She edged closer.

Breath from his open, snoring mouth reached her.

She saw keys; his right arm thrust out across the table shielding them.

Inched…

The man was very deeply asleep. Her arm reached, hand stretched out… Three keys, each longer than her hand, held on an iron ring. Was it possible to pick them up and not make them rattle?

She sucked in her breath. Had to try: extended her arm further. Got fingertips on them…

The keys slid across the table – and ground together. Clinked.

The guard-man stirred.

But his eyes stayed shut. Honey snatched the keys up.

Three keys. Three doors.

Which one to try?

She couldn't, she decided, remember any other windows between Robbie's cell and the latrine shaft. So he had to be behind the first door – didn't he?

If only she could call out his name. She wasn't at all sure.

She wiggled a key into the nearest door lock. It wouldn't turn. She winced as the metal chaffed against her damaged hand.

She switched hands. It didn't help. She tried a different key. Suddenly, there was a satisfying click; the door began to swing inwards – making heart-stopping creaks.

A fetid, awful smell leaked back. Then a guttural snarl.

Which wasn't Robbie. Couldn't be.

Wasn't!

A man, huge, horrible, bloodied, one eye dangling, grimed on his cheek, staggered out from the cell's darkness – and knocked her aside with a ferocious arm-smash. She was flung back. She crashed into the far passage wall, crumpled. Breath knocked out of her, head filled with stabbing lights – light screwed into balls, pounding...

She fought to focus. Where were the keys?

She sucked down air. Tried to fix on the door. The key bunch was still in it. The guard, awake now, but bemused, still dozy, was looking straight at them...

He didn't grab at them.

Or Honey. His eyes lifted to the escaping man.

He'd reached the passageway she'd come up, was stooping to

enter it. Was in – but, almost blinded, his head struck. He stumbled back, swore.

The guard set off, roaring, moving remarkably fast – anger flinging him on. The escaping man, hearing the roar, hesitated, searched back. And the guard was on him, at his legs, dragging him from the passage. Then fists flying.

Honey tried to pull herself together. She might still do it. If she could stop shaking. And think! Because: which door? If she tried the next one along, and it was wrong, what new horror might spring out?

The guard no longer seemed to be winning. The escaped man had rolled onto him...

The air all around smelled of his smell. And the other man's.

She tore her gaze away. Suddenly, what to do had become obvious. People might hear but...

She staggered to her feet, stood between the two shut cell doors, and screamed out Robbie's name.

Where they waited, insects ticked. They waited crouched down in the scrub on the forest's edge. Alice had bitten and chewed her fingernails down to nothing. She said, 'Why can't we go back to the shelter? Light a fire? Honey can find us there. It's where she'd think to go. I really don't like waiting here.'

'How can you say that?' Winn's voice scolded. 'Would you abandon Honey? Robbie?'

Alice shrugged. And for a moment tried to search Winn's face, sought to see if she was not as cross as she seemed – but it was very dark now. And not being able to, she was almost about to apologize – then didn't.

Because, although she had hated Robbie once, she didn't hate him enough now to not want him safe. And sometimes, more and more, she forgot she'd ever decided to hate him at all. But lately, her thinking about Honey had begun to move in the other direction. Honey was increasingly dismissive of her; she'd begun to suspect Honey disliked her. Really disliked her! What she thought now was, she wanted Robbie safe; Honey not so much.

She began to recall instances. Most hurtful had been one quite early on the journey to Burfield's, Winn, struggling to keep up, had fallen behind. She and Honey had been walking side by side; they'd shared a smile, a moment of companionship because they were together and Winn wasn't keeping up. And then, thinking the moment right, she'd plunged in with her question about seed babies. It hadn't taken long for Honey to double up with scornful laughter; then go on – with too obvious delight – to tell all manner of gruesome, explicit details about lovemaking.

Some sounded made up. Some sounded too terrible to believe. She wished she'd asked Winn instead, not Honey. Wondered if she could now?

'You seem to have drifted far away,' Winn said. 'Do you really have nothing to add? In mitigation?'

'It's just that, I think it's stupid to swim in that moat. If she's at the bottom of it now, it's her own fault. I can't stop thinking about the fish and God-knows-what that would be eating her.'

'Somewhat selfish, dearheart. Thinking about what it's doing to you, rather than what could be happening to Honey.'

'Is it? I… I don't want to be selfish.'

'Of course you don't,' said Winn generously. 'You're scared. You're tired. But we must keep moving round close to the moat. Watch for a signal. Listen for a signal – she's a clever girl. If anyone can find Robbie she…' Winn's sentence shattered into a wheezy cough.

Alice shuddered. Looked away from the moat. But the edge of the forest was black as coal.

'If we find them, they'd both better not be dead,' said Alice bitterly. ' Like my father.'

CHAPTER TWENTY-THREE

DEVIL'S CHILD

Honey looked down. Robbie wouldn't.

'We jump,' Honey said.

'It's too high.'

'Men coming… close now. Hurt us – soon now. Brave in crowds… men… like wolves at dusk, isn't it. Jump.'

'No.'

Their words hissed. They were trying not to shout. They stood, wavering, on the battlements of one of the two towers that rose above the gatehouse – Honey looking down at the moat.

But they'd done well to get this far. Fortune favoured – Robbie thought. Them, both. For they'd got out of his cell unseen – and down the first passage too, going in the direction away from the warder's desperate struggle with the one-eyed man. Met no one. And made it to the foot of the tower's spiral-stairs undetected. It was only as they climbed that people began to be about. It proved impossible to get far along the corridors leading off. Each time, they'd had to fall back, back to the stairs. And it became clear that men and woman were searching.

The household had roused. And noise, loud then suppressed, strident then muffled, drove them ever higher – until they emerged onto the tower's battlements; beneath a night sky now beginning to show stars.

There was no one on it. But there was on its twin. One man: eyes fixed on the road. For now.

It was time to decide. Jump or risk capture.

'Must jump,' Honey said. And made Robbie step closer to the tower's edge – and the water.

Where now, he saw, on some of its surface, there was moonlight and starlight sheen – but it remained black as pitch where it met the walls. And it would be necessary to fling themselves into that black, and spring outwards too if they were to be certain of clearing any lip of land that might be at the wall's base. To jump was a sounder choice than attempting to work back through the passages to the gatehouse entrance – if they had to fight. But reason alone wasn't enough. To step out into the air and fall was utterly terrifying. And there was no knowing if the moat was deep enough to absorb their dive – and he couldn't swim.

He reminded her.

Honey jigged up and down, exasperated. 'I help you swim. We jump.'

'I...'

'Must!' Honey shook him, insistently.

He told himself, the drawbridge was raised. If they

survived the jump, if, somehow, Honey was able to get him across to the land they might very well get to the safety of the tree-line. It would take several minutes for the drawbridge to be got down, for men to get out in pursuit.

She squeezed his hand.

They climbed onto the merlon.

They had to get their heels up. Squat, and be up on toes. So as to be able to spring. But, as Robbie positioned his hands, the days of captivity, the lack of food, the exertion of the stair-climb all took their toll. Dizziness churned in him. They were jumping on three, but he was hearing Honey's voice counting down as though through thick fog. On three she went forward; on three he fell back. Consciousness left him.

And Honey didn't meet the water well. And focusing on twisting her body, and then fighting the pain and shock of impact she lost all sense of Robbie.

As she came back up, broke into the surface, something hit her head hard. Water seemed to be in her brain, in her bones.

'I think it's them. Alice quick, quick.'

Winn broke cover, stepped out towards the moat. She'd seen two silhouettes at the gatehouse tower's top. Then none. Heard a splash.

She led Alice. Held her hand. Made her come.

Now men's voices, urgent, harsh, boomed out; Winn heard more splashes – and looking up, caught sight of a bob of arms, heads, disturbance on the tower's top. And guessed that things were being thrown or shot.

Some heavy enough to make the water's surface spout.

She began to run.

'The drawbridge, Winn. The drawbridge!'

Alice had stopped.

'Alice hurry.'

'No. It's being lowered. The drawbridge. There're lights. Lit. Growing. Behind it. Men are coming. We'll get caught.'

'We have to try.'

'No.'

Winn ran. Hoped Alice would follow. But she didn't look back – she would need to harness every breath.

And in moments she was wheezing, then gasping. Her headway faltered, she was staggering side to side, this way and that. The coughs that now came racked her.

But there was something afloat on the water ahead. There, where a slab of darkness slid into moonlight. And then: in the moonlight's patch a shape that was Honey's – face up and drifting. Slight, slight movement of arms, legs drifting it.

But it was deliberate movement. Had to be. Honey was alive.

As Winn arrived at the moat's edge, Honey, almost lifeless now, did too.

But the bank here was steep and the drop down to the water greater than arm's length. Honey was there, but not moving, not trying to climb out. One hand was wrapped into a clump of sedge.

On her knees, Winn coughed up gobs of phlegm, spat them out, cleared her lungs. She lay flat, and stretched and stretched down, and couldn't quite reach. She spoke, but Honey didn't. She told Honey to help, but Honey lay rigid, eyes shut. She said, that if she slid down into the water but couldn't stand up she'd drown.

That the moat would be dug deep enough to make men drown.

She shouted, 'Alice help.'

Alice stood rooted. Watched the drawbridge settle.

From the towers' tops now, loud voices. No more throwing of the stones piled there for the purpose. Shouting instead. To direct: guide the men about to leave the gatehouse.

On the tower, two men lifted Robbie up.

Winn had hold of Honey's leg. Lost it. Then a foot. Ankle. She heaved, frantically. Honey's head disappeared, went beneath water.

'Alice, help!'

The men lifting Robbie paused and disputed ends. Robbie stank most at the head end; the feet end was better.

'Alice!'

They bumped him as they began to work down the stairs. Carrying him was awkward, hard. They cheered themselves by picking the route to the cells that would take them past the kitchen. They would claim there the need for a bucket of water. They exchanged knowing looks.

The drawbridge was down.

Alice thought of a mouth gaping wide. Thought that it was like hell's mouth, flame lurid – the men coming out lit: lanterns and fire torches. She'd made steps towards Winn, taken several back. Wasn't moving now.

Winn hauled. Slipped. Honey's face, just out of the water, sank back.

The searchers advanced.
   Slowly.
   They'd been told to expect some snarling creature of the devil. They'd been warned of shrieks that came out of thickened air. Night's impenetrable dark.
   They knew that Robbie, when first taken, had been sheltering in the house of a witch.

The men came on, cautiously.

Raised voices betrayed terror.

'Alice, please!'

Alice counted the men coming. Five... No six.

'With your help Alice, I can get her. Get Honey. Help me.'

'They're coming Winn. You have to give it up. Save ourselves.'

'Help me, Alice.'

'I can't.' said Alice. And though Winn was now sobbing with the effort of it, coughing and coughing and coughing, Alice turned.

Away from Winn.

Began to run.

In the kitchen.

The pantry-help responded to compliments. And dollops of mutton stew went into the men's hands. Water from a bucket was thrown over Robbie.

Robbie opened his eyes, groaned.

But he couldn't work out how he'd got to be on the floor of the kitchen. He could remember climbing the stairs with Honey, seeing stars, feeling free. He recalled Honey's urgent voice counting down.

Then he couldn't remember.

Alice ran. Tripped, stumbled, fell. Ran again.

Winn had hold of Honey's leg when the men took hold of her. They struck out in rage, punched and kicked her.

The panty-help dripped stew into Robbie's mouth. Taking pity. The men, seeing the gulped desperation, made small piles of the food on the floor. Made him eat it on hands and knees on the floor, like a dog. Made him bark to get more.

Honey was dragged from the water. Crude jokes were made about her nakedness and otherness – and they poked her about. But seemed too scared to keep it up.

Winn thought she heard someone say the devil's daughter lived. But she couldn't raise her head to see. A weapon's sharp edge was pushed against the back of her neck. Kept there.

When a blanket arrived, they rolled Honey into it, covered every part and inch of her, fearful of her words, or stare – her magic. The darkness around them seemed to lump as they did it, and the air above Alice's footfall seethed unknowable. No one had volunteered to chase Alice. No one had suggested anyone should. Tonight the forest was no-go. The forest was not for tonight.

It was an elf-child that had run off – they said.

~

Sir Harry Burfield clapped his hands gleefully together and a smile lit his face and the sword in his hand was put down.

The warder and the steward, watching him, and the dog watching the warder, a low growl sometimes in its throat, body quivering – because of the blood scent, the copious amount of the one-eyed man's blood on the warder's clothes – relaxed. The dog trotted back to its master, nuzzled him. Sir Harry stroked the dog's head. The warder looked down at the bloodstains, as if seeing them for the first time – recollected the knife frenzy that resulted in the kill. The steward, satisfied that the message he'd delivered of the devil child's capture required nothing further of him, turned his attention to the food strewn abandoned across the great hall table – and raised his voice and summoned servants. The warder said, 'A witch, and a devil's child. They must be bound and held separate, and not visited alone. I ought not to be down there with them alone.'

'You have three prisoners and three cells. Keep the doors locked and do not go in. Now get out of my sight.'

When the man had gone, when the steward and the servants were busy, Sir Harry's wife drifted over, gave meat to the dog, murmured and fondled its ears, then said, 'I hope you will not keep a devil's creature here, under our roof for long. She should be examined, convicted, burnt or hanged. She should be lodged elsewhere. She should…'

'She should. But I know that she is not all that she seems. Mary, listen. What we do with her depends on instruction from the Cardinal. I must send word we have her. I must send word tonight. I'll get the letter written now.'

'Harry, not yet. Talk to me. Reassure me. Tell me what's going on. I…' She smoothed out the skirt of her gown, straightened her back, looked him in the eye. 'There have been too many secrets of late.'

'What do you mean?'

'I mean you and the Cardinal.'

'He's been very good to me.'

'Has he!'

He took her hand, led her away from where the servants were clearing, made her sit. He remained standing, looked down at her. Her upturned face caught the candlelight, and she thought it must enhance her pale beauty; she believed that her beauty was absorbing him; that it was a moment to pounce. 'I am your wife,' she said firmly, 'and if there is now a devil in my house then I need to understand what it's doing here. If you imperil your soul, you imperil mine.'

He half turned. She kept her gaze on him; expected him not to meet it. He was master of a lie, but he could not lie to her.

'She is here because of the boy. The boy is here because of her. I would like to be rid of them both, but justice has to be seen to be done.' He spoke, tight lipped. 'I am the King's justice of the peace. I need to remain so. But the boy must be deprived of a platform to tell what he knows. No trial. Thus, delay. My pretence was to keep him locked up to await the sitting of the next Quarter Session. Except, I expected him to have faded away through lack of food long before then. But now, depending on the Cardinal's reply, it may be necessary to make trial here. For all three. Soon. But I will have to send word to the other justices of our shire to assemble; I cannot preside over such cases alone. I doubt that we would need the sheriff to put together a jury, but I will have to use my influence carefully to get the verdict the Cardinal will want. It could be many days. And all must depend on what the Cardinal wants me to do.'

'I see. And meanwhile, we have here a witch and a devil. Shall I send our children away? Sleep my nights in the chapel?'

'Dearest, they are neither of them a devil or a witch. You can trust me on that. Now I must go and dictate my letter.'

'Yes, you must.'

He made his way across the long room. She watched him carefully, took note that his strut and poise appeared undiminished. She took pride in being married to a powerful man; and pride that she'd played a strong part in his rise: encouraging risk taking, smoothing his all too often furrowed brow. But he'd been very secretive of late. And now there was this devil child...

News of the creature had caused pandemonium. Evening dining had been in full swing, and the musicians had just started on something especially pleasing. Then chaos: benches overturned, food and drink, plates and vessels dropped throughout the room. But the fear had been matched by the determination to hunt the creature down. And Sir Harry had quickly brought matters under control.

He controlled them. She controlled him.

She let out a sigh. Felt contentment easing back. The pulse of the musician's tune she allowed space to dance in her head. Hummed it a little and smiled.

But just as her husband was leaving the room a man she did not recognize entered. He handed something over. Spoke – something. 'That changes everything,' she heard Sir Harry say.

CHAPTER TWENTY-FOUR

THE CHAIN

A pigeon was flying. West. London towards Wales. Message attached. The code-symbols: 'take care' and 'be ready to hide'.

For the widow who lived with her brother in the house on the Southwark end of London Bridge had, after a sleepless, troubled night, decided to set the chain in motion. Her brother had told her he'd heard that the King was back in bad temper, and thus unpredictable. And that it was to do with a Sir Lionel somebody, Cardinal Wolsey, a princess from some far away land. And Bristol merchants – and witchcraft.

She had no idea how there could have been connection made to witchcraft. But there it was: stark and out there. And one thing could so easily lead to another.

Hysteria.

Accusation.

Sham trials... executions.

She'd made ready the pigeon to fly at first light. But then hesitated, saw it must take wing into a clouding sky. Dawn, arriving, was brushing the clouds pink as dog roses: the ominous country-folk's shepherd's warning.

She offered Saint Christopher a prayer.

The message was written on parchment she'd scraped thin as a fingernail; the outside she'd coated in wax and rolled only when certain it was dry. But it could, nevertheless be destroyed by heavy rain – which might very likely descend. She whispered – lips pressed to the bird's cooing head – go strong, Fortune favours the brave.

And let it fly.

CHAPTER TWENTY-FIVE

MATTER IS GOD

At Burfield's, rain fell heavily. And Alice, leaving the shelter of trees, fearing that the forest would shortly be searched methodically to find her, shuddered as heavy drops landed on hair and shoulders and quickly damped through to her underclothes. She thought, never in life have I been this miserable. But she no longer cried. She had cried over and over, wandering all of the night, keeping to the forest's edge, keeping sight of Burfield's – because it was where Winn was, and Robbie was. And where, she supposed, Honey lay dead.

Round and round and round. Held to Burfield's like a moth to a candle flame, not stopping, not resting. She'd told herself that with the first glimmer of dawn's light she'd begin to journey home – that she couldn't for the life of her understand why she hadn't done it days ago. That Mummy would rouse and help.

Yet still she'd hesitated, not wanting to walk away from the place where Winn and Robbie were.

But what could she do? What!

She told herself she had run last night from Winn because someone had to stay safe. Stay free. Convinced herself. For how else could help come, rescue come? How could it?

What Alice told herself was, I was right to run. And her crying eased whenever she visited this – and then determination to put things right came to stir her. But the anxiety of what to do next, what would be for the best, returned and returned. Overwhelmed her. Made thinking numb.

That she'd go home was the only plan that stuck sufficient to keep returning to. She reached the road.

Coming up it was a cart, an ox pulling and a man with a long whip encouraging the ox to lean harder into the wooden collar sat on its neck. Alice froze. Indecision filled her. Run – or go on? Walk nonchalantly forward, or sprint for the trees? Which? Oh which? And then she thought, how like last night – and revisited that.

And the cart was upon her.

'Hello. And good day to you, miss.'

The man, not young, not old, face streaked with dirt where rain had worked on it, smiled and lifted his hat. Alice warmed to the smile – it had a rascally look. Mummy, she thought would have called it that. Not exactly a someone-to-trust look, but someone who would not do you harm.

Rascally.

Alice smiled back. 'Do you have any food?'

The man raised eyebrows expressively. 'Food fit to share with an angel? I don't think so.'

'I'm not an angel.'

'Could 'ave fooled me. Hop on the cart. There's room between the barrels.'

'I'm going the other way.'

'So am I – just as soon as I've delivered this ale to Sir Harry's. That big place behind us.'

'I know it.'

'Do you now.'

The man made as if to go on. Alice made up her mind. Climbed up.

'So breakfast is brown bread and ale. For us to share sweetheart, just as soon as my cart's load's been delivered. Then I'm going your way. A free ride in exchange for your excellent company.'

As they covered the last few yards of road before the drawbridge, Alice reminded herself that Winn had come to Burfield's because she believed that the safest place was the lion's den. That no one would think to look for them there. And she would stick to the cart-man as if she were his shadow – stick to him like glue. She felt sure he wouldn't care.

The drawbridge was already down. The great oak doors it fronted were open. The man led the cart onto it, over it. She sank down as low as she could get between the barrels and waited for the sentry's voice to inquire.

There was no voice. They passed through the enclosed gatehouse entrance and into the courtyard. No challenge came. No voices of any sort. Just the rain beating down.

'It's like the place is under some enchantment,' said the carter uneasily. 'There are always people about.'

Could that be? Alice followed the carter across the courtyard towards the small door that allowed entrance, down a short flight of steps, to the retainers' kitchen and hall. Her heart thudded and the possibility took hold that Winn really might be a witch? A real one. Disciple of the devil sort – with power to raise storms, upend the natural order, leech energy, sow sleep.

That she could, seemed suddenly very possible: and she was excited and horrified in equal measure. For if all were under a magic spell, then Winn and Robbie would be free.

But the devil might be there too.

As they banged down the kitchen steps she expected Winn to run out at them. Or that the devil would. As the carter pushed open the kitchen door she thought her head must explode.

He entered. She followed. This was the servants' kitchen, next to their eating hall. There were always going to be people there. At this time of day.

It was empty.

The fires were lit, there were pots set to boil, piles of bread removed from the bread ovens cooling. But no one person. Not a single soul.

'Come on.'

'Where?'

'The passage. Go down it. There must be someone somewhere about. I'm going.'

He seemed more irritated than fearful. She let him leave, but after several moments of hesitation ran to catch up. To warm by the fire and eat bread was the greatest temptation – but she couldn't face being alone.

He heard her coming. Waited. Put his fingers to his lips. As her panting eased she heard from somewhere ahead a faint murmur of voices like a buzz of meadow insects. He seemed confused by it. She shrank back. He took hold of her hand.

'It'll be all right, girl.'

She felt her hand squeezed, but his words hadn't been said with much conviction. He dragged her on.

Outside the entrance to Sir Harry Burfield's great hall they discovered the end of a long line of people. Alice recognized some of them: Burfield servants she'd met yesterday whilst trailing around behind Winn. The carter, clearly, knew many more.

The ones at the back explained. They'd been summoned to make testimony. The entire household. Sir Harry's clerk was writing down witness statements, to compile substantial evidence of witchcraft. He expected everyone to have something convicting to say.

'But not us, girl. We're getting out now. Witchcraft, eh! We'll unload the ale barrels, roll 'em to the kitchen door. And be gone.'

Mary, Sir Harry's wife, stood a little way back from the business end of the witness line, but was carefully observing, listening – and her face, suffused with satisfaction, beamed. And Sir Harry looked up at her for a long moment, took pride in her being there, though it risked letting his attention slip from guiding, probing, cajoling – which she'd determined he must do even though his clerk kept saying he oughtn't, that he mustn't put words in their mouths. Mary, noticing his gaze fixed on her, sent back a smile and a nod – which reinforced his conviction that he should take no notice of the clerk's protests. For this was her idea and plan.

He, coming late to bed, had been consumed by rage and anxiety. Wolsey's messenger had said that the boy and the two girls must be killed. At once. Tonight. Tomorrow. Latest. Do it.

But he didn't see how. As a general rule, he wasn't against sanctioning murder in the national interest. All the most affluent city-states in Italy these days were, apparently, recommending it. And the papal state was one of those. So if our very own Cardinal says to do it, then surely God won't mind – Mary?

Except: not in his own home. Where rumour of murder would be hard to suppress. No. There had to be the veneer of justice.

She'd lit the candle by their bed, sat on the bed's edge, eased him down so that her legs embraced him, held him against her. She kissed the top of his head. And as the tension began to leave, as his anguish waned, she told him that all he had to do was compile evidence enough that the girls were powerful witches. Thus, establish that it was too dangerous to let them live. For once night returned they might break loose from the strongest chains. So, gather a great mass of testimony: eye witness proof of their terrorizing. Then proceed with ordeal by water. That very day. Hanging could follow if, by not drowning, they made obvious their power. The boy too, then, as their accomplice. For already they had demonstrated extraordinary evil.

Justification would be, the need to settle matters before today's light went.

For Alice's mother – a different plan.

Wolsey's man explained it to Matthew. Grumpily. Because his legs and inner thighs ached and ached. He would give his right arm, he said, never to get back on a horse. But he had to ride on now to the place of the witch called Winn, check that she hadn't returned there. Her and or the American savage. Or Alice. Which was why, he, Matthew had to kill Sir Lionel's wife.

He stared into Matthew's face. Looked for any weakness: anticipated a glazed blank of thoughts struggling, face paling – desperation, prevarication there. Matthew held the look. His eyes blinked back bright, excitable.

Matthew said, 'It will be as an accident. A fall down the stairs. I'll get her to come to the tower, break her neck, then push her down. Everyone knows she is no longer in her right mind. Everyone knows. It will be simple as wringing a chicken's neck.'

'Sounds too simple.'

'No, simplicity's best.'

Wolsey's man watched Matthew go, then walked wearily across the courtyard to the stables and his horse. He had arrived long before dawn and had no choice but to wait for servants to be up and about – for the main gate to be opened. His nerves were exhausted; he jumped now at the slightest sound.

He'd hated being out alone in the dark.

Arrived, down off his horse, the coin dipped in holy water, given to him by Wolsey, he'd pressed and pressed against his lips as he might a rosary. But it hadn't helped. In the dead hour just before dawn his every thought had fragmented, blurred – as if atrophied by enchantment. He'd felt clogged up, deadened: as if evil beings were burying his hopes and belief under dirt. His horse stomped and pulled and would not settle.

He stroked its ears, nuzzled its face to his chest, but it wouldn't give back comfort.

The eventual arrival of sunlight was brief; clouds thickened and rain fell.

But some positivity had returned. It was the bailiff who'd been first to go out from the manor house – hurrying, taking big strides, anxious to begin chivvying the villagers to get working on the fields. For it was the time of year when the green shoots of sown crops were raising fast, and weeds, if not pulled out, would rise faster and choke them – he said. And consequently, he – the bailiff – spent the briefest time possible establishing credentials: the proof that he truly was about Cardinal Wolsey's errand: on a long journey, in need of sustenance – for the horse and himself. Hastily, the bailiff pointed out the stables and kitchen. In the kitchen Matthew had been located. Matthew then, confidently, extemporized a need for them to be able to be together outside. Just them.

Since the rain began to fall, matters had proceeded auspiciously. The omens were better and better. As he heaved himself back into the saddle, the clutches of wicked enchantment receded into dream.

'Sounds too simple.' Those three words rattled around Matthew's head as he walked back to the kitchen. Because, in all truth, it was only simple if Lady Catherine could be roused from her bed. She had been reluctant to engage with the world ever since her daughter had gone missing. Two days ago she hadn't, apparently, risen at all. Thus, the message he wanted delivered to her now had to involve Lady Catherine's maid.

Which was eminently possible. It was obvious that she, Agnes, the maid, had an interest in him. But she wasn't his type – at all.

As he expected, Agnes was loitering in the kitchen. She was greatly motivated by food: her plumpness was unusual in a serving girl – but she made use of every opportunity to eat whatever was going spare. He grabbed up some freshly baked bread and gestured to her to sit beside him on the kitchen table's bench. Making sure the cooks and helps were busy, he broke off a lump and placed it in her mouth. Her fleshy lips sucked momentarily at his fingers. He pulled them away with obvious, deliberate slowness. She shuffled closer. A leg pressed against his.

Again he made certain the kitchen staff were focused on their tasks. Then he leaned towards her and kissed her.

Her face registered only the briefest moment of surprise. Then she kissed back, thrusting her tongue into his mouth. He found it hard not to respond. The very last thing he'd expected was to feel aroused.

He pulled away. Breathing heavily. 'Not now. Not here. Later.'

'And that would depend.'

'On?'

'Your intentions. Towards me.'

'Those will revolve around what happens next.'

'Really. I wasn't born yesterday.'

'Not yesterday. But not so long ago.'

'I'm not a child.'

'Prove it.'

He stood up, stood behind her, put his hands on her shoulders, bent and whispered in her ear.

What he said was, tell your mistress that tomorrow is the feast day of Saint Augustine. Remind her that he was the first ever Archbishop of Canterbury. Tell her that in Kent, where I grew up, the country folk say that anyone who gazes out towards Canterbury on the days just before Augustine's day and prays, and invokes Augustine, can nudge Fortune's wheel for the better. And say that the tower window, not the one that looks south but the other one, looks out towards Kent. That it's the straight-as-a-crow-flies way. And that it must be done while the sun is low over Kent – like now.

'Why?'

'Because, sweet girl, the sun is matter and light and heat – and matter is God and light his son and heat the Holy Ghost. The sun, thus speeds the passage of prayers.'

'Well I've never heard that.'

'Where you born in Kent?'

'No. But…'

'But? Look, do you trust me or not? Just tell her…. I'm just trying to do her and us some good. And don't tell anyone else.'

'Trying to get into Lady C's good books?'

'It'll be all the better for us if I do.'

It took close on an hour for the response he sought to happen. The longest hour of his life, he thought. But he was sure she would. Her desperation was such that she would clutch at any straw. The flimsiest straw...

He tried to distract his fear by working on different ways to convince Agnes to tell no one. Lady Catherine had been for a long while now teetering on madness's edge. No one would be surprised to find that she'd fallen, distracted. But there would be an inquest. Agnes must say nothing. He imaged holding Agnes hard against him, kissing her face and telling her. He imagined fondling her body and telling her. Making it glass clear, that Lady Catherine's broken neck was an accident. But fingers would point and accuse if she mentioned the Canterbury stuff – and they'd never get married, then.

Not ever – Agnes.

As he thought on, and worked at fiddling with this and that, anything that would keep him in the vicinity of the tower's stairs, he reminded himself that he was Burfield's man, and that Sir Harry would reward him well. And that Sir Harry Burfield was the Cardinal's man, and the Cardinal was the Pope's. The Pope understood best, the will of God.

His conscience could rest easy – couldn't it?

When the steward, Tom, passing by, asked him what he was about, what he was doing there, he answered smoothly, only the duties of the common man to God and Christ, and laughed, and ignored him. Tom shook his head sadly and went on his way. Not ever the sharpest proverbial blade of the weapon rack, our Tom – he thought. And was thinking it still, when Lady Catherine, suddenly, appeared.

She strode past him briskly, didn't seem to register his presence at all. And fear of failure shot through him, and he shook and couldn't stifle it. If Agnes hadn't told her… Or she had and wasn't believed… If she wasn't going to the tower…

His legs worked clumsily as he tried to follow. His eyes seemed to find it hard to tell him what he was seeing. For several moments it was as if he moved through swirling fog. He shook his head hard, blinked and blinked. Tried to regain control. Thought about similar stuff done before, when people had died and he hadn't been caught. Told himself, this would work out. This would be no different.

She just had to enter the tower.

Not walk on past.

When Lady Catherine reached the stairs and began to climb, the fear left him. To see his plan beginning to work out drove him confidently forward. For I'm as clever as any of them, he thought. All the lords and ladies and stewards and Agneses. All of them.

He moved faster. He checked that no one else was about. He could hear the swish of her clothes as they brushed against the stone of the steps, the clump of her shoes, a growing, laboured breath. He, placing each foot softly, proceeded upwards with careful deliberation. He edged into the top tower room only when he heard her praying.

Agnes looked for Matthew. The kiss they'd shared, tugged at her; when, as now, she ran her tongue over her lips she could taste it still and her body tingled pleasurably. Matthew. He wasn't especially handsome – and young no longer: in his beard she'd noticed a streak of grey. But she was often drawn to laugh at his snide remarks, she admired his cussedness, understood, she believed, his reason for surliness. She thought his independence brave. She wanted to kiss him again. Now.

But he was nowhere to be found. She had risked Tom's wrath to be in parts of the house where she oughtn't, she had rushed Lady Catherine through her dressing. Still, for all that, she believed she'd delivered Matthew's message to Lady Catherine at a propitious moment. The moment Lady Catherine sat up in bed and asked if Alice had yet come home – and before she convulsed into predictable floods of tears. And – before the now usual refusal to get out of bed; to just lie motionless, staring blankly. Not responding to anything at all.

But she'd shown interest in the suggestion to go to the tower – today.

The tower was the last place Agnes thought to look for Matthew. She hadn't thought he'd go there: because Lady Catherine might.

Because of the rain outside, the passage leading to the spiral-stairs that accessed the two turret rooms of the tower was gloom-dark. The opening onto the stairs held a pool of deep darkness. Agnes was reluctant to go up. She'd never done so – and the servants often told tales of a ghost that wandered there.

A woman's ghost.

But that would be between midnight and the dawn. Not now.

She sucked in a breath. Listened carefully. Went up one step. Two. The air around her seemed full of tension – like, she thought, hot and still summer's air in the moments before a storm.

Another step.

She listened, harder still.

Nothing.

She decided Matthew wasn't there. That she'd check outside now, try the stables.

She heard a shriek.

Just for a moment. A momentary desperate screeching – that suddenly cut off, stopped so fast that already she wondered if she'd imagined it. But if she hadn't, then it could very well be Lady Catherine that had made it. In the place she'd encouraged her to go.

Agnes decided. Went up. Battling the ache in her legs that pained from almost at once. Panic drove on her heavy limbs.

The first flight ended. She paused, gasping. The room off it was empty. She climbed again, her breath rasping out.

Matthew, his hands at Lady Catherine's neck and mouth, trying to stop her making noise, trying to get her head to an angle where he could twist it and snap bone, didn't hear Agnes. Lady Catherine was proving stronger than he thought she could ever possibly be: her legs and feet, elbows and hands had pummelled him. But he was on top of her now. His hands finally in the place to do it.

Agnes blundered in. Saw the commotion. The frenzy.

And flung herself forward, swinging her hands at his head, slapping then fisting. Her blows battered, knocked him off Lady Catherine. He turned, faced Agnes.

He charged at her. Hit hard, fists clenched, pounding into

the soft flesh of her stomach, where her ribcage stopped. She doubled over in agony, fell. Couldn't protect herself as his feet kicked her head.

The kicking suddenly ended. Blood was in her nose, her mouth. Ribbons of it ran down over her eyes.

But it wasn't her blood.

Agnes pushed up onto her knees. Matthew was sliding down against a wall. From his throat, blood arced out in a fine spray, long streaks of it were smearing onto the dust on the wooden floor.

Lady Catherine wasn't on the floor. Somehow she'd got up, taken hold of one of the ancient swords in the wall-rack, swung it with all the strength left in her.

CHAPTER TWENTY-SIX

RUN

The rain stopped. But first it had fallen in great drops, malevolently, making them walk bent backed, close to the ox. The hide of the ox steamed.

Before the rain finished, the wind gusted and the trees flanking the road soughed oddly and were knocked about. Then, thunder crackled, and the lightening streak that brought it came down just ahead, and Alice had shrieked in terror. The cloud there, extraordinarily black, was piled high as she could see – and behind her, it seemed to reach down to the ground as if purposely. As if, purposely, she'd thought, cloud was swallowing Burfield's up.

But now, wonderfully, it wasn't. For in the time it took to agree to go to the back of the cart and push, while he, the carter, lent onto the edge of the yoke and pulled, so that they could get away from Burfield's faster still, the sun slid in, the black swirl diminished, became fragmented grey and watery white – then more and more, the sky was blue.

And all that came sudden enough, making contrast enough, that Alice now, as she pushed, pondered miracles –

and wondered if Good Fortune was finally taking a firm hold of her hand for the better. And, having prayed thankfully a little, she asked about breakfast, and making a fire so that they could speed the drying of their clothes.

'Whatever, sweetheart.'

But he didn't stop. Only looked back at her, uncertain.

'Is it that you want to get even further away?'

'Can't be too careful.'

'But I have to eat now. This is the hungriest I have ever, ever been.'

He stopped the ox. Without warning. She, pushing still, slipped and her chin and nose bashed into the cart's back. Her nose bled.

'Look! Look what you've done. Look!'

He shook his head laughed.

'I took you for a good man.'

He walked towards her. 'Sweetheart. Good you value, is it?' He said carefully, 'Reckon it's for the good that I should teach you some manners.'

His eyes stared hard. She saw menace in them.

'You'll be sorry if you hurt me.'

'Is that so. Understand, lass, I am not in the habit of taking instruction from a mere slip of a peasant girl.'

'I'm not a peasant.'

'You're clothed like a peasant. Are grubby as some peasant. Smell like a peasant.'

'But I'm not.'

'And I'm the King of Egypt.'

'I don't have to explain anything to the likes of you. And if you know what's good for you, you'll do what I say.

Understand, I'm the daughter of a great man and a great lady, and you are to take me home. You'll be well rewarded when you take me home. But first I want breakfast. I demand breakfast. Here. Now. This is far enough away from Burfield's. We're quite safe.'

His tinderbox sparks lit twig, and twig lit sticks but the fire only smouldered and wouldn't blaze. He asked her to help gather more firewood, find dryer stuff, but his tone was surly, never deferential, so at first she wouldn't and then, when she did, she moved sluggishly, muttering that she was too tired, too cold. Getting the fire to flame tipped the cart-man's patience, angry swear words burst out of him. He threw at her the bread he'd broken, laughed as she missed the catch, laughed as she scrapped off it rain-wet and dirt. But there was plenty of ale, and he offered that conciliatorily. She drank and felt brighter, better. The cart-man drank, became more settled.

Sitting as close to the fire as she could bear, she watched dreamily the wet of her sleeve steam, and began to make pictures in her mind from the shapes the rising, transitory wisp-trails suggested – which was something she did often with clouds. For clouds stared and stared at, could turn into the strangest things… the oddest things. Beautiful things.

She thought of angels.

She said, drowsily, 'When you met me, first, you called me an angel. Have you seen one?'

'No.'

'Not even your guardian one?'

'No.'

'Oh.'

'And I don't waste time thinking about what I don't see.'

'Well I do, and you should, so there! Angels... God's messengers, our guardians. Fighters of devils. Powered by God's love. You do know they are ether, seen solid? Ether... the pure air that surrounds the heavenly spheres?'

'Do you know, that words run out of your mouth like flux from an arse? More ale?'

He watched carefully. When her eyes closed, he took hold of the leather drinking cup, eased it from her fingers. He used his arms to pillow her head down to the ground.

Lay her on her side. Legs curled.

On the fire a log collapsed and flame spurted. And he made up his mind.

Wolsey's messenger sent to Bristol said, 'Waste no time. Just get it done.'

'Kill 'em both?' muttered Rog. 'Even the woman?'

'That's it. Got to. All to die. 'Spect they're snuffin' out Sir Lionel's wife as we speak. Caution, chuck to the wind. Make it look like robbery. Get on with it.'

'Good,' said John.

''Bout bloody time,' said Gregory.

'Just so long as Wolsey'll cover our backs,' said Rog.

'Usually does,' said Gregory. 'Even the King – 'spect.'

'King supports the Cardinal for certain,' said John.

They checked their weapons.

They crossed the road shielded by a passing cart.

Rog, casually, opened Robbie's parents' front door.

Alice stirred. Was coming awake. But still the dream: a spider crawling from her ankle up her leg. She hated them – spiders large or small – and her every fibre was telling her to brush it away and she couldn't. Even as the dream faded, the pressure of the spider remained, and it moved to her thigh and she knew she must open her eyes now.

Now.

But she didn't. She realized that the cart-man was kneeling next to her, hands on her, rucking her clothes up. The cart-man's hands: kneading, stroking. She lay rigid. Rigid with shock and fear. But she knew something had to be done, that she had moments only to do something. Stop him.

What…?

She jerked back her elbows, raised her head, chest, opened her eyes. As her head came up she saw the side of the cart-man's bent head, saw his ear, brought her mouth to it, bit down hard. He shouted out, tried to shake her off, punched hard. Her teeth sliced and bit, deep, deeper, it filled her mouth…. . He flung her off.

She landed next to the fire, almost in. Its heat fierce.

She got to her knees. The cart-man was examining his ear. Blood and bits of it were on his fingers, on his beard.

In her mouth.

She reached out to the fire.

Sparks splattered up as she pulled a branch out, she shrieked as its hotness scorched her palm – but she didn't let go. The burning end of it she thrust towards the cart-man. He jerked back. She leapt up. Ran.

Robbie's home occupied three levels: downstairs held the

business room with its counting table, and the kitchen with its great fire; on the first floor were the living rooms; on the second, bedrooms. The business room was right by the front house entrance but it was empty; two male servants were preparing food around the great fire – getting up the stairs proved easy.

Rog went first, John last. John kept a little way back; watched them. Gregory lost all nervousness once action began; Rog was never one to hang back.

John was happy to let them do the killing. It would be messier, noisier left to them, but the servants in the kitchen appeared engrossed in their tasks. And there were, still, carts rattling by in the street.

Alice ran, tiring fast. The burn of her hand throbbed and throbbed, her blistered feet brought pain in every foot press. The cart-man's shouts kept coming and were louder. Closer. Now, she could hear his feet slapping down on the road.

She knew not to look back over her shoulder, knew that it slowed her. She was certain that if he caught her, he would do to her the terrible things men did to women – the things that Honey, laughing and laughing, had just two days before told her about.

Then, murder her.

'Dragons. See.'

'What's that dear?'

'Dragons, Rowland. Robbie's favourite thing… to draw. Robbie's…'

Rowland saw his wife's face crumple. Then recover – pulling herself together. As he expected she would. Because she always had – as long as he'd known her. But an unusually wild gleam in her eyes remained – troubled him.

His Jane, wife of twenty years, standing beside him both figuratively and actually, next to a small table where he'd asked her to be, was, over the last few days, far, far from being the woman he knew. Relied so very much on.

The table's top was covered with red and black cloth of good quality. On the cloth stood a newly purchased globe.

He was pleased and peacock-proud of the globe. He'd hoped that showing it to Jane would offer her distraction.

His globe – his commission. Crafted from every available Spanish and Portuguese source.

Just arrived, extravagantly expensive – which its creators claimed would instruct a particularly accurate portrayal of the 1520's world: with the Americas, the New World, marked out, on Rowland's instruction, especially colourfully. But almost at once, Jane's finger had rested on a phrase writ large across the eastern coast of Asia: 'Here be dragons'.

It wavered over it now.

Plaintively, she said, 'It seems to me that English dragons are back. That monstrous worms are at large. Slithering about. Here. Where is Robbie, Rowland? Where is Bright-as-flowers? And Alice's father? And Alice? Dragons are here, Rowland.'

There were tears in her eyes. Tears were unusual too – almost never there. She was a woman of considerable inner strength. Rowland, hesitantly, because he was not used to doing it, having to do it, placed a consoling arm across her shoulders. He said, with all the encouragement he could muster, trying to squeeze the lump from his throat, 'Robbie's bright as sunshine. Strong as your famous resolve. Gets it from you. No harm will come to him. I still believe that he and Alice have simply gone off together, are getting to know each other better. Doing... well... you know... But if Bright-as-flowers isn't found. Or anything happens to her... then our hopes for this New World, so enticingly drawn here, will be dashed. To pieces.'

'Bright-as-flowers was to be our bridge in wasn't she?'

'Bridge... road... Whole new beginning. Our way back to Eden.'

'After we find Robbie, we can try harder to find her? Find out where Sir Lionel's taken her?'

'We will, dear... Christ!'

A man he did not know was in the room, sauntering forward, casual, face filled with a big grin. 'Nice globe,' he said. 'Must 'ave cost all of a purse full of pretty, pretty pennies.'

Rowland took a step towards the intruder, intent on shielding Jane. Rowland had a knife in a sheath attached to his belt. He could see that the grinning man did too. 'No other globe like this in existence. But what's it to you?' said Rowland, trying to size up the danger – which suddenly, alarmingly increased: there was a second man.

Rog groaned.

Gregory was supposed to wait. Supposed to let him get right up close to Robbie's dad. Gregory hated to wait.

Gregory slid in as if he were a miracle play actor on a stage, legs and arms spread wide. 'Gotcher,' he said.

Jane screamed. Not hysterically, but in furious anger. 'Out!

220

Get out of my house!'

'Make me.'

Jane flung the globe.

Rowland pulled out his knife.

The globe missed.

Rowland's knife jabbed. Rog parried the thrust, smashed down the arm, clamped on. Twisted it.

Pain streaked up Rowland's arm. Rowland cried out. Swung with his other arm...

Gregory's knife came up under Rowland's unprotected ribs and entered Roland's chest. Rog, laughing, let go. Rowland fell forward, his weight wrenching the knife from Gregory's fist, impaling himself as he spread onto the floor.

Rowland twitched once and lay still.

Gregory and Rog stepped away, sucked in breath. Shared a look. They knew Jane was running, had reached the stairs. But they assumed that John was there. Would stop her.

They let her run.

She thought there'd be other people travelling. Travellers from Burfield's – surely!

She'd seen no one.

And the cart-man was so close. She could hear gasped breath.

Ahead, twenty, thirty yards, there was a slight bend in the road. The forest edge straggled almost to it. And she thought something large moved there. Animal, man peeing, robber waiting? Something... which, suddenly, was a man, stepping out now casually, slowly onto the road, taking the direction to Burfield's, not looking back, not looking towards her. But seeing him gave her renewed hope, a spurt of strength. She lengthened her stride, went fast, faster – but she knew she couldn't maintain such pace for many yards; already her legs were giving out, her shuddering breath almost gone.

'Help me… Wait… Please…'

He didn't seem to hear. He walked on – as if lost in a world all of his own.

'Please.'

The man paused. Turned slowly. She staggered towards him, hardly able to stay upright.

'Help… me.'

The man stopped. She lifted her gaze to his face.

The face of a leper stared back.

CHAPTER TWENTY-SEVEN

GUILT

From out of a woad-blue sky, a dot, which became a bird, which he – Wolsey's man – watched. Because he'd explored, though somewhat perfunctorily, the remains of Winn's house, and some of the ground around it, and had quickly concluded she wasn't returned there – and so he was disappointed, tired, bored.

He watched the bird. It was a pigeon. He was not an admirer of birds, though he was happy enough to hunt them, trap them, but he took note now, thought the pigeon's flight clumsy if compared to most.

He watched.

And the pigeon swooped suddenly down, and before it disappeared into the trees on the clearing's edge, he caught sight of a momentary gleam from its leg, as if a candle had flamed into life there – and because he had nothing else to do, he walked across in the direction it had gone.

Pushing his way between branches, looking again skywards, he saw what appeared to be a very small child's hut mid-way up a beech.

A child's hut? Or fairies'?

And the awful fear from the night returned, surged through him. And he felt as if all the trees at the clearing's edge had taken a step closer, and the sky was sinking down.

Jane was in the street. John was there too. But walking away fast, looking back only through glances snatched as he paused outside a fish-seller's. She was crying for help, imploring everyone's help, seeking to raise hue and cry.

Succeeding.

A man and a woman jostled past. And he could see others, suddenly many, emerging from the neighbouring buildings – clustering around her.

But she wasn't pointing at him.

He hurried on. Reflected. That if she'd cried out on the stairs she'd now be dead. But she hadn't – and so he hadn't. Because, when she'd seen him there, waiting, she'd met his eyes, held the look, continued to step down, forward, controlling her fear. She'd placed a hand on his arm reassuringly. She'd whispered, 'You don't want to kill me, do you? Do you?' And he didn't know why – why he couldn't. But instead, he'd bent his head, kissed her hand – then descended the stairs, keeping ahead of her and not looking back. Walked away.

And, walking on now, he sensed still the trembling grip of the hand on his arm, the shake beneath the breath of his kiss. And he thought that he would strive forever to remember it. Because it was a moment, shocking, in which the good in him had been triggered – and he was sure that it was that something supernatural had nudged hard.

He'd shown mercy and was glad. So perhaps God's mercy would be shown to him. Ask and you will receive – wasn't that how it worked?

He wondered if he should now enter a church and ask. A new start – pray for it. This very day.

The meeting, in the courtyard, because everyone knew that witch-magic worked less well anywhere open to the sky, began with prayers. Then Sir Harry, shrilly, while holding up examples of written testimony, summarized.

And the household, assembled – all there save the warder – were swept sharply towards the overwhelming likelihood of their having been exposed to witchcraft. For earlier, some had told of inhaling when walking along corridors a biting odour of sulphur – others, at times, a smell so bad that it could be nothing less than the putrefaction stink of hell. And on top of this, there had been several sightings of a black cat wandering close to Robbie Walker's cell (significant because devils could appear in the shape of cats, dogs, toads – even bears). And many of the manor's younger men and women had described peculiar sexual desire, long repressed, in recent days reawakened – and of dreams saturated with horror. On the night of the appearance of 'the girls' – Sir Harry explained, controlling his words, bringing the tone of his voice much lower – which was also the night of the prisoners' escape, a gibberish incantation had been heard by several of the kitchen staff. And now careful examination had revealed, on the secret places of the bodies of both girl captives, odd marks that suggested initiation by the devil's claw – evidence that they had, at least once, attended a witches' Sabbath.

Now Sir Harry paused, letting the startled, murmuring crowd explode into fearful noise. He glanced across to his wife for reassurance. She nodded, and stepping closer, ran fingers up his arm, hand to shoulder, and over his neck. Then she eased his head nearer, and with her lips against his ear told him that she was proud. Proud!

Now, with one hand, he removed his wife's from his neck, pressed it gently, let it down by his side. His other hand he raised. Waved about. Signalling silence. And waited – and only when all at last were, he settled himself to explain what now had to be done. Harnessing the slow, explanatory language he'd honed during his ten years as a judge, he reminded them that he was first and foremost Justice of the Peace, appointed by the King, honour bound to follow every expected procedure. And yet, the evidence gathered that very morning was sufficiently wide-ranging to indicate beyond reasonable doubt, that all three, the boy and the two girls, were dangerous servants of the devil – and, therefore, that their execution ought not to be delayed. Nevertheless, in order to make absolutely certain, to have investigated beyond reproach, there would be, within the hour, an ordeal by water. 'For,' he said, 'it is widely known that in water, witches float – because they have renounced baptism. And thus, if they do – float – then no power in the land should seek to overturn my, our, judgment. What we must do next, will surely be accepted by all. If they float we must hang them – and hang the boy.'

At Winn's, Wolsey's messenger abandoned his wait, climbed onto his horse and without a backward glance rode hurriedly away.

CHAPTER TWENTY-EIGHT

WORDS

The leper walked, keeping to a slow pace, seemingly unconcerned. Next to him, Alice. The cart-man, a respectful distance behind. Following.

Alice couldn't seem to find any words. Her breathing had normalized, her legs had stopped shaking, but her mouth, trying to open, shaped to a thin, tight line, and her tongue twitched – the sounds she thought to make stayed in. She looked around her, at the trees on either side of the road, at the cart-man behind, the sky above. She didn't look at the leper and she didn't think he was looking at her.

Her father, she recalled, had once told her about people he'd fought beside so traumatized by the shock of battle that they could no longer speak. Sometimes for hours. Sometimes, days. Sometimes… But it was a mistake to even begin to start thinking about her father. At once, in her mind's eye, remembrance of his severed head flashed – and then she found herself thinking that the corruption she'd glimpsed of his dead face and the lumped deformities on the leper's face were horribly similar. And she stole a look at the leper's face – and shuddered. And the shivering that set in up and down her spine, she couldn't make stop.

But what should she do? What? She felt too dazed to think. Too tired. Burfield's place was fast approaching. The cart-man was behind her still. What?

And then a new thought struck: that the man, the leper man, hadn't yet spoken to her, hadn't asked her anything at all. And anger welled up in her and dampened her fear, and she said angrily, 'Am I too young to talk to, look too stupid to talk to? Am I too dirty to speak with? Or care about? You've said nothing at all to me. Nothing. Why is that?'

'Good morning.'

She pressed.

'Why?'

He stopped walking.

She looked up at his face, flinched, but was surprised that the words that came now weren't monstrous – as she thought they must be, would be. Surprised that they came gentle, calm, with a rhythmic lilt.

'Dear child, I have long thought it best not to begin a conversation unless I am spoken to first. Some people believe that hearing a leper's words can pass on the illness. And, until your outburst just now, you haven't spoken to me.'

'It's just that, I didn't know what to say.'

'And yet there must be a great deal that needs saying. The man following? Is he your father?'

'It's just that I couldn't think of what to speak… because… because you are a leper.'

'Is he your father?'

'No.'

228

'I see.'

Walking resumed. The same leisurely pace. As if, she thought, he had all the time in the world…

But, she reminded herself, she didn't. Burfield's was already close enough for her to be able to make out the hair colour of a watcher on its gatehouse tower.

Alice said, 'The great house up ahead, like a castle. Is that where you are heading?'

'I am taking the road to it, yes. Then going on beyond it. To a leprosaria, a leper house, that is tended out of the charity of a nunnery.'

'Leprosaria… And have you travelled far?'

'I have.'

'Are there not many such places?'

'Not now. Once. Outside almost every big town. But very few are needed now. The disease seems to be fading away, fewer and fewer sufferers with every year that passes.'

'Because fewer people are embracing evil and being punished by God?'

'Not at all. Leprosy can infect the most saintly of people. Indeed, many say that our suffering exists to hold a mirror up to the suffering of Christ. And that, because we endure purgatory on earth, in death we shall go straight to heaven.'

'So not all bad… but you don't have a warning bell? Or leper's clothes? Why is that?'

'The bell is not just for warning. The ringing of it is also for those who wish to give charity to us to hear us when we come. I, however, prefer to hear only the fall of my feet on the road. And the song-chatter of birds. It frightens them – the bell.'

'And the clothes?'

'Don't like green. Don't like beaver skin hats. I refuse to hide my face under a hood.'

'I ran from a leper once. He had a hood. It was after I ran… after that, that the bad luck started.'

A breeze cut down the road, and her tears slid cold on her cheeks.

CHAPTER TWENTY-NINE

WHAT ALICE SAW

Some hundred yards from Burfield's gatehouse, Alice and the leper watched. Watched people, kitchen staff, house servants, armed retainers, and boys, girls, emerge out of it. Saw bubbly bounce in their step, apparent cheerfulness on faces, heard their talking rising, falling, rising again – excited sounds. Happy as gatherings on Mayday or Twelfth Night's morning – Alice thought.

The cart-man watched too, just a little way from them.

And then the leper noticed, coming down the road, down the part they had yet to travel, more people. Small groups. Burfield's villagers, the leper suggested. Coming to join the whatnot.

The whatnot. The whatever. For it seemed the oddest thing to be happening. They didn't think it was a feast day, holy day. It wasn't Easter – most certainly, it wasn't the beating of bounds.

Odd.

So they watched.

And the people from the manor house and those from the

village began to meet, coming together at a point about half way along the west side of the moat. A small boat was on the water. Alice's eyes were drawn to the boat. She could see it clearly, the water around it bright, the sun high overhead, the battlement shadows shrunk back.

Two men were in the boat – one was kneeling up, using a paddle, keeping the boat in a place close to the gathering crowd.

Was the crowd's gathering, Alice wondered, something to do with the boat? Was the boat finding something, rescuing something? Someone drowned perhaps? Except, if it were a drowning, would the crowd be cheerful?

Was… was it Honey!

As Alice thought this, just as the shock of the possibility surged through her, a man at the back of the crowd turned his head towards the gatehouse, waved an arm in its direction. In moments all had turned, were looking there. And, some, towards them.

Alice cowered back behind the leper, sank down into the rain-wet grass – grass high as her knee when standing. She lay on her side, knees to her chest. She wriggled to force the grass over her, make herself disappear. If she could only disappear…

'Look girl. Watch, watch. See.'

She lifted herself, peeped out at the crowd. They weren't looking at her after all. Or the leper. Their eyes seemed fixed on the gatehouse. Expectant. Waiting.

And she breathed more easily. And then thought, he's with me. The leper. Helping me. And I don't even know his name.

She hadn't asked.

He hadn't said.

Why hadn't she asked?

Kneeling up, she said, 'I'm Alice. My name is Alice. Yours?'

'William.'

'I don't know why I didn't ask before. I…'

'People often don't. Don't see me as a person. Someone with a name.'

'I… I'm sorry.'

'Good. But shush now and look there.'

She looked properly. Out of the gatehouse, over the drawbridge, a procession snaked: a priest, Sir Harry Burfield, six others well dressed, then a small cart, dragged by two men, pushed by two more. And in the cart, sitting on its floor were Winn and Honey, ropes holding them – back to back.

I know them,' Alice said.

'Probably not for much longer.'

'Why not? What's happening? What? What?'

William reached out to take hold of her hand, but she shrank away from it. She heard him sigh, but kept her gaze from his face. So he sat down in the sodden grass beside her, gestured she sit lower, waited until she had – and explained. She listened, then wouldn't, clamped her hands to her ears, whimpered. Muttered. But he kept on, repeated, keeping his voice calm – and, bit by bit, enough of it sank in. Alice absorbed the probability, likelihood, that Winn and Honey would shortly be attached to the middle of a long rope, pulled out to the moat's middle, that once there the rope would be allowed to slacken, that they would be judged, that judgment would be based on how quickly they sank under. And if… if they didn't sink, then they must be witches. And burn or be hanged. Though, if they were left under the water for too long they might drown – which, however, apparently, was unusual unless those charged with manhandling the rope were particularly stupid. More worryingly, William added, he had heard it said, though he thought no one, surely, could be that dishonest, that the rope was sometimes manipulated to aid floating and thus ensure guilt. Ordeal by water – but he'd only heard about it, had never seen it. 'Don't look, don't watch,' he said. 'Just pray. To favourite saint. Every saint. That they don't float.'

Pray! She tried to protest, tell him he was mistaken, had to be – but her voice made only wheezes of anguish.

And in her head her mind cried, shut up, shut up, shut up. And she ignored him and watched. And saw that the cartman had moved, was following the procession.

And the predicted scene unfolded.

The procession moved very slowly, deliberately slowly, to cruelly stretch the prisoners' apprehension – and feed the crowds expectation. And when, finally, the cart reached the waiting crowd their howl of anger was frighteningly rapacious, predatory – but people moved quickly back and away, didn't surge, surround it as Alice thought they must. And the crowd then fell almost silent – just subdued murmurings drifting over, like the intoning of prayers in a church, but quieter. Noisier – as Honey and Winn were dragged out of the cart, forced to stand.

Alice saw that their legs were free, but their hands were tied behind their backs. Alice could see that one end of a much longer rope had been taken over to the house side of the moat by the boat, that the two men were now out of the boat, holding the rope, that some of the rope was being wound around Honey and Winn. Alice saw, because the crowd had been scared back by her friends' arrival. But with the rope secured the crowd edged nearer, spread round, closed off Alice's sight.

She could see no longer.

She ran to the moat's bank, tried to locate them – still couldn't. She anticipated a splash, expecting them to be dragged in. Waited.

Waited. She realized the crowd's noise had stopped. Now she could hear one voice. A priest's sing-song. Latin phrases – she thought.

Then William's voice. He was beside her. 'Look, look.'

'I am looking.'

'Not that way. This.'

With great reluctance, not wanting to move her eyes for one second from where Winn and Honey were, she swivelled round and followed William's hand-point. And saw Robbie.

CHAPTER THIRTY

❦

THE HANGING TREE

Men led Robbie out. Three men. Through the gatehouse, over the drawbridge, out of the building's shadow, onto the road. The sun came hot onto his head. The road's wet-earth smell lifted up into his panting breath.

He walked slowly, reluctantly, went forward only because points of sharp metal jabbed at him. He had strength enough to walk because he'd been brought a substantial breakfast.

Only when he'd finished eating had the warder explained. When he'd chewed the last mouthful and gulped down the last of the ale, the warder had told of what must happen. With a voice that cackled with cheer: that Robbie was to be hanged that very morning, that they didn't want him to be so weak from lack of food that Sir Harry be blamed for maltreatment of prisoners. That he was to be hanged just as Winn and Honey were being dragged into the moat.

For if witches they were, their powers would be focused on saving themselves.

Robbie's hands were tied. Ahead walked an armed man.

Behind him came two more.

Which ought really to be quite sufficient, Sir Harry had said. For there would be no onlookers as all were by the moat – and the prisoner would have to walk just a hundred yards to the tree.

From the tree, three ropes slung around a low branch. Three nooses, waiting. And the hangman.

CHAPTER THIRTY-ONE

DEATH-TIME

Alice looked along the moat's outer edge towards where Winn and Honey were. She looked over to Robbie. Back towards Winn. To Honey. Telling herself, imploring herself to do something. But what – and who first to save? Who? Shocked, distraught, the thought went round and round her head. Who to save? Then, how?

She clenched her fists, forced herself to reason it out. The crowd, perhaps a hundred people, were gathered around Honey and Winn. Honey and Winn weren't yet in the water. Water held no fear for Honey. Death might not be there for them yet. But Robbie...

Robbie was nearly at the hanging-tree. Stopping. Going forward a pace. Stopping. Trying desperately, desperately not to get there.

A new thought stirred, that Winn and Honey were not yet condemned. Robbie was. And that was so very much her fault. She had begged him come. She had...

No. No. None of that mattered.

No. She told herself, what she must accept was the change

that she knew was in her. That oddest of new feelings – that tingled easy as breath.

A lover's love – she supposed.

And thus, it was Robbie that had to matter most. Robbie she must save.

Robbie…

How?

She told herself she would think of something. Somehow… She began walking towards him. Towards the tree where they were leading him. She would… what?

She felt a hand push down heavily on her shoulder. She stopped. Half turned. Made herself look directly at the leper's face.

'Where are you going? What are you doing?'

'To rescue him.'

'How?'

'I don't know. William. William. I don't know.'

'You said my name. Thank you for saying my name. People so often don't see I have one. That, I am.'

'Well, I do see. I do. Help me.' She reached out, took his hand. Pressed her fingers against its course hardness, misshapen lumps. 'Help me.'

'But why? If he is to be hanged he must have done wrong?'

'He hasn't.'

'You don't know that.'

'I do.'

She softened her hand's press. Brought a palm up to touch his cheek, spread her fingers gently, then let the fingers sink down a little way into his beard.

'Please.'

'I could... Might... I have an idea that might get us very close. But you will have to let me carry you, hold you – be lifeless in my arms.'

'Yes.'

Robbie had almost reached the tree. Alice allowed herself a last quick look, then closed her eyes, tried to make her body go limp as William lifted her up into his arms and started to carry her. The odd smell and feel of him she pushed away.

She focused on his plan.

His plan was to enmesh their curiosity, so that he could get close, within grabbing distance. Then he would drop her down and then... well that he couldn't predict. The men might run from him as some did, try to hurt him, as some did. But there would surely be distraction. And he might then do something. Or they – he and she – might do something. Some something to get Robbie away.

What?

William, clearly, was very strong. He seemed to be carrying her effortlessly.

'What the devil-shit are you?'

'Just stop there. No closer.'

'Stop there. Stop or be run through.'

William dropped Alice. As she hit the ground, she opened her eyes, saw that she was feet away from one of the guards, rolled at him, lunged forward, swung her legs so that the impact crunched his shins – and toppled him. And as he fell, missing her just, there erupted above her shouts, grunts, the grappling heaves of William and the second guard.

She looked up. She saw the second guard-man flung back savagely, and strike the hangman, bring him down.

A knife landed near.

Alice rolled over to the knife.

The man she'd felled got to his feet, shot Alice a look of contempt, moved towards William.

Alice stared at the knife. Long bladed, heavy. Took hold of it. Looked for Robbie.

He was slumped on the ground, dazed, eyes blank. He said nothing, didn't help to bring his arms up so that she could get at the rope. She had to do it.

Must help William! Must help William! Must help William! The silent shout, rattled in her head as if it were hollow. Crash, crash, ear to ear as the rope frayed, snapped apart. Must help William...

She handed Robbie the weapon. And she saw recognition arrive in his face, saw the blankness pass, like a solitary cloud's shadow – saw the glint of determination back in his eyes. He jumped to his feet.

William, somehow, had appropriated one of the guard's swords, was swishing it expertly, keeping back two sword-armed men.

And the hangman.

And the sword-less guard

All circling. Quick, lunging movements. Spitting insults. Eyes on William.

Robbie strode straight at the hangman. Alice went for a leg – and as the man, suddenly sensing Robbie's nearness, focused on Robbie's attack – got to it, clung on. Clung – even as, with his other leg, the man kicked hard blows. Her body writhed with the pain – but Robbie got under the swung fist, got the knife to the man's throat.

'Stop or he dies. Stop!'

The guards hesitated.'

'He dies, you die,' said one.

'I have nothing to lose. Put down your swords.'

They didn't have to. William stepped forward and knocked them out of their hands.

In the lee of the hanging-tree, hidden from the crowd, William and Robbie tied the men together. Gagged them. Alice watched. Her heart hammered, her chest heaved.

'We must go to the monastery. Where I was headed,' William said.

'We must try to rescue Winn and Honey,' Alice said.

'Child, we cannot.'

'But we must!'

She looked about her, at Robbie, at the onlookers by the moat, at the sky. She rolled her eyes. 'Please.'

William shook his head. 'There's nothing we can do here. Sanctuary can be asked for at the monastery. It's the best we can do.'

'No, it isn't,' Robbie said. 'Honey in water swims good as any fish. We can give her, them, a chance. Make distraction. At the top of our voices, we shout. Make the crowd watching them chase us. Then run for the forest.'

'What do we shout?'

'Shout, cowards.'

They shouted. Sucked in breath. Shouted again. Three times. Alice a fourth. The crowd seemed not to hear.

Then three crows, down in the grass close to the crowd, flapped disturbed. And as they rose and cawed, Alice murmured, they clapped their great ragged bat-wings up – but didn't know why she said it. Where she'd heard it.
    And then a man turned. Then a woman. Another.
    'Cowards!' shouted Alice.
    And the stampede–chase began.

Under the water, five, six feet down, with the rope purposely slackened off to make them sink, Winn and Honey hadn't heard the shouts. But the boatmen holding one rope end had. And the men holding its other end had. And as their attention shifted, and the rope stayed slack, Honey took her chance and kicked out hard, rolled to get on top of Winn, keep Winn down. Smaller, lighter, Honey hadn't been able to get Winn to hold herself as she needed her to. Winn, unable to swim, convulsed with panic from the first moments off the land, had writhed and flapped and gulped water. They'd sunk, surfaced, sunk again. But now with Honey above her Winn's held breath burst – her struggle faded. She began to drown.
    Honey didn't.
    For when the ducking rope had been tied about her she'd placed in her mind an image of a blow snake, brought it, held it, caught the moment when a blow snake, threatened, flattened its neck, pushed and puffed up the head as if the neck's mass had been transferred there. And – thinking only of the snake's head growing larger, neck shrinking – she'd

filled her lungs, held the breath, made her chest big, expanded, stretched her ribs. And although her wrists were separately tied behind her back, she'd managed to keep her arms, from the elbows up, pushed out too. The rope wasn't wound as tightly as the men intended.

Now, under the water, she pushed out her breath, wrenched her arms down, kicked swimming strokes with her legs, wriggled her body out of the rope's grasp. She surfaced, snatched a breath, bent her legs up to her chest, sank back towards Winn.

Winn seemed to be without life. The rope weight was keeping her down, and she was limp, unresponsive. Honey, keeping her back turned to her, gripping her with her legs, tried to tug at the rope, loosen the binding – but her own hands were still roped behind her back, she couldn't see what she was doing. Couldn't... She twisted up to stare into Winn's face – there seemed to be nothing there: no spark, glimmer, existence. Nothing. Just eyes wallowing. Drift of hair

Winn, she was sure, was dead.

And the big rope now was tightening, dragging Winn back to the moat's surface. The rope-men were back on the job. Honey leg-swam away – relieved. She couldn't save Winn, but Winn's death might save her. Absorb attention, stretch time – aid escape. Winn's death, Honey thought, would be for the best. It was the way of things. The time for life, the time for death.

Winn's death-time had come.

CHAPTER THIRTY-TWO

SEE THE KING

Alice woke. And the woman – Sister Beth – sitting beside her, looked down at a face flushed with sweat, saw wide eyes that seemed not to register, that looked beyond to the high ceiling. But then, for a moment, Alice seemed to breathe more calmly – and Beth wondered if it was because she was hearing the song-chant that had begun to drift in, making a way over the cloister's lawn, from the chapel – where her sisters were at worship. For Beth believed their music to be a potent, soothing, reassuring sound – voices together, harmonizing sometimes, singing praise. With healing power attested by other patients, certainly.

And – Beth thought – most certainly, singing communally had always lifted her. Thrilling to the plainsong chant as it passed between voice-parts – though then, usually, she found it impossible not to smile. Smiles of joy, not embarrassment or nervousness. Joy – though sometimes she'd be told this was out of place, the subject-focus too serious. But even then she'd smile – and risk penance: which, just now, was her infirmary duty.

And so, believing even without small doubt, that hearing music's devotional beauty could impart profound delight, and thus lift the afflicted back towards health, she determined to arrange for the infirmary door to be left open, the chapel doors too – whenever sung worship happened.

And prayers quite often when it didn't – for Alice's fever lay deep, and prayers seemed very necessary.

For many days, Alice scarcely heard Sister Beth's prayers. And didn't manage, very often, to accept the sips of water, the herbal brews, the pulped food. But the singing sometimes penetrated her delirium, slowed its nightmare swell. And song was the first thing to occupy her thoughts the day the battering ach in her head eased and the temperature subsided. She lay still but relaxed, tautness gone – and some of the music sounds recently heard she worked up into matching the rhythm of now regular breaths. Music stirred Alice, connected her. For the echo of it was, she thought, a familiar happy buzz – as of a bee humming, or birdsong sometimes, or the insect drone noticed when first entering woods. Or... well she wasn't sure – but suddenly she thought that if she explained it to Winn, hummed to Winn the buzz, Winn would explain.

She sat bolt upright – to ask Winn.

'Where's Winn?'

'Who is Winn, child?'

'I want Winn!'

'There's your mother, and Robbie, and Robbie's mother, and Honey and William. There is no one called Winn. Here.'

The temperature came back

But on and off and on, Alice murmured about the music.

Music, said Beth, is food for the soul.

Music said Beth – on another day – is… is… So there's this bit in Bede's Ecclesiastical History of the English People that follows on from writing about much huff and puff destruction by barbarian types, Picts and the like, that talks about how a churchman named James, a deacon, brought peace to York and increased greatly his Christian flock because he was very skilled at singing.

Muttered Alice, Winn would know. She keeps pigeons, and pigeons coo it.

On a day when Alice's temperature seemed less severe, Beth brought visitors. One at a time, only. And each met an unresponsive, grave face, but somehow managed, having been warned it might be so, to sound cheerful. And Alice, looking up at them, did so without surprise as if it was obvious they would be there – and when drowsing more, the faces came to her filtered, as if looked at through a veil. Or mist. A fog. The words spoken floated fogged too, detached from their speakers. Though, after they'd gone, she remembered the part in each explanation that seemed most relished. And sometimes these flipped about in her head, and became sometimes merged together, and sometimes broken and created anew – and sometimes replaced the Latin words of the music that entered from beyond the infirmary door, taking possession of its chant, meeting the cadence, seeking ownership. For some deep instinct seemed to be telling her that she mustn't lose the remembered words – that whenever they began to fade she must fight to find them. That they mattered. That she must let them lie on her tongue keen as pepper-taste.

William had talked up how he'd carried Alice to the nunnery after she passed out; Robbie'd dwelt long over how it was his idea, his cleverness, that they hadn't run far into the forest, instead climbed up suitable oak trees, let their pursuers pass by, then doubled back to the road – where Honey, coincidentally, found them. Sister Beth told of how the Abbess granted sanctuary, sent word to a particular, trusted abbot, and that his message had quickly reached the King. Robbie's mother expounded the greatness of her husband's bravery; Alice's own mother: how in self-defence she'd killed a man. Honey boasted of the cleverness of blow snakes and her skill in not panicking in the water – unlike Winn.

Winn...

Alice, waking early one morning, feeling better, watched the rise and fall of dust in the sharp beams of sun and all of a sudden remembered how unhelpful she'd been to Winn in those last days. The others too. But especially Winn.

And a little later, when Robbie and Sister Beth were sitting with her she sat up and said she'd finally remembered one of Winn's stories, told to her on the journey to Burfield's. That it was one she'd been trying to remember. Winn told it because she – Alice – was troubled about the existence of Honey's gods – couldn't understand how there could be other gods. How they caused Honey to be. Then Winn told the story.

'Which one?'

'The bat-wing one.'

A girl-child on the cusp of adulthood, fresh as trees just into leaf, skipped out over the meadow, fringed the beech wood, reached the stream. A fish leapt out, and water drops flicked and glimmered like stars – and a bird, bathed with sun, feathers rainbow-bright, flashed past the fish. And the fish, when back in the water, sang but wasn't heard. And the light-bird in the air sang, and was. And a crow, black as night, wings ragged as a bat's, watched from a tree branch – and joined the light-bird's song.

Light-bird. Dark-bird. Two singing. Same tune – different sound.

The girl puzzled it. The tune was in her head: it was a tune she'd heard many times before. But not the sound… that different sound…

'So I don't remember properly how Winn told it, but the girl wanders village to village, through tree lands and hill lands, asking why. Some say this. Some that. This-words and that-words. Sometimes: that-words and this-words. Words so many … her head spins giddy, her feet pace frenzied – and she trips and falls. Then someone – I forget who… been trying so hard to remember – tells her a new word, the word made flesh. Says it's made vital by searching heart, not head.

For there the key-song is. Heart not head. Where God placed it.

'The heart-heard song – Winn said it was. Heart-heard. God's tune in all of us, waiting to be sung differently.'

Robbie frowned, sucked in a breath and let it out slowly. Sister Beth drew breath to speak, glanced at Robbie, stared severely down at Alice, said, 'Oh...' but then didn't press on. But the fingers of one hand rubbed hard at the other, and her body wriggled as if shaking off something crawling there. Alice seemed not to notice, only looked at Robbie, her face seeming more relaxed than he thought he could ever recall – as if all fret had been rinsed clean.

He said, 'The heart first, not the head? Sounds like something that charlatan Martin Luther might say.'

'Who's he?' said Alice.

'A dangerous monk,' said Beth.

'Oh...' Alice sat up, alarmed. 'But can a monk be a bad man?'

Beth leaned over and took hold of Alice's hand, squeezed hard. 'Shush child. All people are complicated. Temptations abound.'

'Which is why, sometimes, even popes go bad,' Robbie said.

'And kings,' Beth said.

'Let's hope our one isn't. We, Honey and I, and you – yes Alice, you – have been summoned to an audience with the King the very moment we are able to travel.'

❧

'I'm afraid you cannot see the King. The King is in France. And when he gets back he is intending to visit the West Country and spend the rest of the summer hunting. You can't see the King here.'

'But… but…'

'There are no buts.'

'Oh, but… there are. There are…'

So many good reasons, Robbie made to say. So many. But the man – the sergeant-porter, no less – had a stern, red-flushed face, which now thrust imposingly close, and Robbie's protest withered. Then for a long, strange moment he found his skidding thoughts braked only by the man's redness: pondering if – Alice-like, he suddenly thought, alarmed – the flushed red was the result of too much morning beer or too great exertion of trying to make himself heard over the hubbub?

Such hubbub.

The noise and dazzle of the great hall-space: Westminster – royal palace: boasting rooms of much gilded, painted, stencilled sumptuousness: walls bright with tapestries and panel portraits. Meeting place of Lords and sometimes Commons too – with a courtyard nestling a clock tower. And chapels of astonishing grandeur.

It had left Robbie overwhelmed, floundering.

But impressed. Such an extraordinary, ancient palace place. Westminster. Where also the Court of the King's Bench, Court of Chancery, Court of Common Pleas had sat. And where everywhere, in every possible part, shops and hawkers and musicians and acrobats shouted exuberant noise powerful and loud as Bristol sea waves surging up a beach – Robbie thought.

'Walker you said? Robbie Walker. There... there is something for you. Please wait here.'

'But...'

The man turned and left.

'But, please...'

Failing to prevent the sergeant-porter leave, Robbie felt anger slap – then pricks of tears. Because, since his imprisonment, the cocksure assertiveness that had once been almost second nature he'd struggled to regain; every day, now, he felt diminished.

Every day, now, too, he felt cross, angry, his temper on short fire-match.

Struggling.

And the size and pace of London he was struggling with particularly. And today: Westminster Palace.

He looked quickly behind him to check that Alice and Honey had remained where he'd told them, not witnessed his confusion. He'd said, keep a discreet distance, watch the entertainers – he'd said it was better if he stepped forward to explain without Honey as a distraction.

Except that, that wasn't it at all. He feared he wouldn't be able to cope. And he hadn't. It had never occurred to him that the King wouldn't be in London for weeks and weeks. It hadn't occurred to him to check.

It was failure nothing less than humiliating – he thought.

Though, perhaps, there was still a chance, he'd some moments now in which to marshal the argument. When the sergeant-porter returned he must – must! – make clear that the King himself, via the investigators sent to Burfield's, had told him to come to the Westminster court – and to bring Alice and Honey. He had to emphasize that point. And then, then he must explain that only the King would do, that it was the King he must see – because he wanted the grant of a charter to allow him to trade with Honey's people. It was he who'd last seen the map that contained sketches, so he believed, of the coastline of the lands of Honey's people. Thus he, Robbie Walker, who'd help rescue Honey, ought to be the one sent out to return her to her people – and hopefully win over the friendship of her father. Honey's father – a sort of king. Who'd sent his daughter to England to learn about England's King.

He, Robbie Walker – explorer.

The possibilities danced in his head. And he didn't see that Honey and Alice had come to stand beside him until Honey nudged him.

Each took an arm, each pressed reassuringly as, falteringly, he explained.

'What now?' said Alice.

'I don't know.'

'Back to Bristol then, isn't it,' said Honey.

'Only for a little while…' Robbie said. And then, determined to ease – seeing it stark in Alice's eyes – their disappointment, dashed hopes, he made effort to rally, pull himself together. Told himself he must, for her, for Alice. He said, more cheerfully, 'Which won't matter. We are going to be very busy. I've a shipping business to learn to run. A wedding to plan. You, both, to protect – until the King gives us permission to set sail. And then a ship to find, a crew to hire and a voyage to edge-of-the-world lands.'

Alice sighed. 'You have it all mapped out, don't you.'

'Maps are a favourite thing – remember?'

'I really don't think they're mine.'

'They will in ti…'

Time. Which seemed to have stopped. For though close by people were jostling and laughing, some making first-meeting exchanges, others reuniting, and across the room all manner of sounds clashed or mingled, none of it registered in the minds of Robbie and Alice and Honey. Because Winn, Winn herself walked, limped and coughed her way to them, and embraced them. And wouldn't answer their relentless questions. Not yet. For the day for that would be later – less it return too painfully her terror. Spoil this moment. Even thinking it. So she didn't explain that with Honey apparently escaped, Burfield could not risk her death. And so his servants had pummelled her chest, breathed their own breaths down her nostrils and mouth, over and over and more, trying this and that, every which way, and pumped medicines in to make her sick water up. And how then, when revived, she had been locked up, hidden – and freed only because the King's men, acting on information received, had made an unexpectedly thorough search. And…

Winn, beginning to cough, broke free of the hugging. And Robbie looked eagerly at Alice, and Alice at Robbie – and they exchanged a smile.

Winn said, 'World's starting… to find its way again. Robbie and Alice together. A something needing to be.'

Author's Note

Robbie and Alice – *a Tudor adventure*, was started when lockdown began: unable to tutor one of my homeschooled pupils (a thirteen-year-old girl), I wrote it to compliment her interest in Tudor England, sending a chapter at a time – her encouragement powered the story on.

Thank you, Maisie.